STRANGER
ON THE RUN

Also by Marilyn Halvorson

Cowboys Don't Cry

Let It Go

Nobody Said It Would Be Easy

Dare

Brothers and Strangers

To Everything a Season

STRANGER ON THE RUN

MARILYN HALVORSON

Stoddart

AN IRWIN YOUNG ADULT BOOK

Published in 1992 by
Stoddart Publishing Co. Limited
34 Lesmill Road
Toronto, Canada
M3B 2T6

Canadian Cataloguing in Publication Data

Halvorson, Marilyn, 1948–
Stranger on the run

ISBN 0-7737-5532-2

I. Title.

PS8565.A48S8 1992   jC813'.54   C92-094964-9
PZ7.H25St 1992

Cover Design: Brant Cowie/ArtPlus Limited
Cover Illustration: Greg Ruhl
Typesetting: Heidy Lawrance Associates
Printed and bound in Canada

*Stoddart Publishing gratefully acknowledges
the support of the Canada Council,
Ontario Ministry of Culture and Communications,
Ontario Arts Council, and Ontario Publishing Centre
in the development of
writing and publishing in Canada.*

To Dan,
without whose expertise
I would never have been able
to destroy a D7

Acknowledgements

The author wishes to express appreciation to the Alberta Foundation for the Arts for its assistance in the writing of this novel.

STRANGER
ON THE RUN

One

I drove south that October afternoon. South into the welcoming arch of an Alberta chinook — and out of the lives of the only people who cared if I even stayed alive. And the ache of loneliness inside me swelled up into a lump in my throat so big I thought it would choke me.

I laughed at myself. Big, tough Steve Garrett. King of the loners. Half an hour down the road and you're homesick. Come on, Steve. You did a better job of running away when you were twelve.

You can't go home again. That was a famous line from somewhere. Now I knew it was true. But, I'd almost got away with it. I'd found out where Pop and Beau were living, got myself an honest job training horses, and spent nearly two months there. Long enough to get close to Beau, to remember what it was like to have a brother. And to meet Raine. Raine who was so much like Tracey . . .

No, I couldn't start thinking about Tracey — or Raine either for that matter. I had enough to think about. Like where I'd go. How I'd stay out of jail once the cops found out it was me Romero was shooting at.

Carlos Romero. He must want me pretty bad to have come all the way from Vancouver himself to kill me. Getting mixed up with him was the worst mistake I'd ever made. But when you're a hungry fourteen-year-old street kid it's hard to turn down good money for delivering a few packages — even when the money's from a dealer like Romero.

Things changed, though. By the time I'd turned eighteen I'd met Tracey, fallen in love, and grown up enough to realize that if I planned to live to see twenty I'd better start changing my life-style.

But Romero asked me to do just *one* more delivery and I really needed the money. That's when I got busted and went to jail for six months. And that's when Romero promised to watch out for Tracey for me till I got out. He watched out for her all right. When I got out on day parole three months later I found out she was dead — OD'd on cocaine. But I'd stake my life on the fact that she'd never touched the stuff before.

I never went back to jail. Instead I set Romero up for a bust — a bust he managed to slither out of like the snake he is — and ran for my life. I'd been looking over my shoulder ever since, running from Romero, running from the law.

Now, Pop's gutless truck was sweating its way up a long hill. I reached over to shift down — and sudden hot pain shot through my right arm. At first the bullet hole had been kind of numb but it was getting over that. Funny, when I was a kid playing cowboys and Indians I always wondered what it would feel like to get shot. Now that I knew I'd just as soon let it stay a mystery. I'd picked up a knife slash or two when I hung out with a street gang in Vancouver, but this hurt different. Not a whole lot worse, just different. I knew the wound wasn't serious. It had been a small caliber pistol and the bullet just tore through the muscle and out again. Probably wouldn't be winning any arm-wrestling matches for a while, though.

Raine's red scarf was tied around my arm for a bandage. "The scarf's a loan, not a gift," she'd said when I left. Did that mean she really wanted me to come back some day? But why would she want me back in her world after the way I messed things up between her and Beau? After the way I messed *everything* up.

The road ahead blurred. Angrily, I wiped my sleeve across my eyes. Come on, Steve, get serious. You're not gonna start cryin' are you? No, it's not that. You're just tired and you've lost some blood and . . .

I was still trying to get myself to buy that lie when the Chevy finally struggled over the crest of the hill. And, right there, coming up the other side, was a shiny blue and white car with red and blue lights on top.

For a second, my heart quit beating completely — and then it took off at a dead gallop as a rush of adrenalin tore through me. Every muscle tensed, ready for action. But then, a sick emptiness flooded through me. Action? What action? I was a sitting duck. If the cop wanted me, he had me. In my old Charger, things would have been different. There wasn't a cop car in Alberta that could follow its taillights — I'd proved that the hard way last summer. But in Pop's lame truck

I took a deep breath and made myself stare straight ahead like I hadn't even noticed the cop. Trust me. I'm just a good ol' boy, straight off the farm, listening to Ian Tyson on the stereo and headin' home to feed the cows. I had one thing to thank the Chevy for. I sure hadn't been speeding.

The vehicles slid past each other with a soft swish. My

eyes locked on the cop car's image in the mirror as it climbed, hung silhouetted against the sky for a second, and then disappeared over the hill. How soon would it happen? How long would it take him to slow down, turn around, and come screaming back down the hill after the truck his radio had warned him to watch for? Year-long seconds crawled by as the Chev seemed to move in slow motion. Then, it happened. A vehicle topped the hill behind me. My stomach knotted and my hands clenched on the steering wheel as the silhouette took shape against the sky. Big, rounded . . .

It was a gas tanker!

I started breathing again but I was shaking all over. Just ahead, a campground sign pointed to a sideroad. I turned in, relieved to find the place deserted, let the truck roll to a stop behind a grove of spruce, and cut the engine.

I don't know how long I sat there, staring out at the passing traffic, my mind numb, my body so tense it ached. A few cars went by. And a couple of horse trailers. One belonged to Ken Glover from High River, probably hauling home Redeye, a big, honest bay gelding I'd ridden every day for nearly two months — including today when I'd ridden him into the sale ring at Kincade's Quarter Circle.

I sat there long enough to be pretty sure the cop wasn't coming back. Long enough for the short October afternoon to start sliding into dusk. But I couldn't hang around here forever so I forced my mind away from the past and started trying to figure out my next move. I took out my wallet and counted the bills. Ninety-two bucks. Not a whole lot but I'd got by on a lot less. But once I hit Calgary I'd be without transportation. I'd promised Pop to leave the truck for him. And even if I hadn't, I couldn't keep driving it. Sooner or later the cops would start looking for it.

So, what it came down to was ninety-two bucks and the clothes on my back. I laughed, thinking of the two hundred and fifty dollars' worth of new clothes I'd finally bought from my last paycheck after Beau'd threatened to shoot me if I wore out one more pair of his jeans. All those new clothes were neatly packed in a duffel bag in the trunk of my Charger back at the Quarter Circle. I'd known I'd have to hit the road today. I just hadn't counted on it being quite so sudden.

So here I was with just a jean jacket between me and an Alberta winter, a jean jacket with one sleeve soaked with blood. Yeah, I was gonna be real inconspicuous.

On a hunch, I took a look behind the truck seat. Sure enough, Pop had left his old red plaid jacket in the truck. I would have kissed him right then if he'd been there. That jacket was the best break I'd had all day — which says a lot for the kind of day it had been. I started to put it on but then had a better idea. I got out of the truck and headed down to the shallow creek that flowed through the campground. Shivering, I unbandaged my arm, took off my jacket and shirt, and washed the blood off my arm. Then I took a good look at the damage. There wasn't much to see.

Just a couple of little dark holes, oozing a bit of blood. I washed them out as good as I could, grateful that the cold water numbed them some. Then I washed the shirt and jacket. The bloodstains didn't come out completely but the cloth was dark enough it didn't matter. The holes in the sleeve weren't anything spectacular. A catch on a barbed wire fence could have made them. I washed Raine's scarf about a dozen times, trying to get it clean — until it occurred to me I still needed it for a bandage anyway.

I rebandaged the arm and tried on Pop's jacket. It was a couple sizes too big — Pop had kinda run to belly since he got middle-aged — but things could be worse. I buttoned it up, collected my shirt and jacket, and headed back for the truck.

It was getting dark now, dark enough that no one would notice my laundry drying. I opened the passenger window, stuck the ends of all four sleeves inside, and rolled the window up good and tight. As I pulled out onto the highway and began to pick up speed the shirt and jacket billowed out like the sails on a clipper ship. They'd be dry by the time I hit civilization.

I drove on south, watching the mountains turn into black paper cutouts against the chinook arch and trying to make some decisions. I hadn't thought any further than getting to Calgary and ditching the truck before it got me picked up. But then what? Stay there? No, it was too close. Vancouver? That was the place I knew best. But there was nothing there for me now but people who wanted me dead and a memory that made me want me dead, too. Where, then? The States? No, crossing the border was too risky. East, then? No, I didn't . . .

A break in the engine rhythm interrupted my train of thought. There it was again. It was missing. It jerked, spluttered, missed again. I steered for the shoulder. As the engine gave a dying wheeze I checked the gages. No! I couldn't be out of gas. Not now. That kind of thing was so dumb it only happened in the movies. Bad movies. But, as I stared disgustedly at the gas gage, I had to admit it. This was one day of my life that wasn't about to win an Academy Award.

I slammed my fist against the steering wheel. This was so stupid — and so logical. Pop had just driven in from halfway across Alberta and then headed straight over to find out what was going on at the horse sale at the Quarter Circle ranch, where I was working. Of course he hadn't stopped to fill the tank. But, I hadn't thought of that. Never once even thought to check the gage — until it was too late.

Hitch-hiking time.

I collected my still-wet clothes, locked the passenger door, started to lock the driver's side, and then changed my mind. Knowing Pop, I figured there'd be no way he'd have the foggiest clue where his spare keys were, so I stashed this set way back under the seat and left the door unlocked. With luck, any hopeful truck thieves would be too lazy to search and too stupid to hot-wire.

I'd just started walking when a set of lights came over the hill. I stuck out my thumb, hoping that if this guy wouldn't give me a ride he'd at least try not to run over me. He went right on by. Then the brakes squealed, and the left brake light came on. I guessed the right one was burnt out. The rusted old half-ton that backed up beside me looked pretty well burnt out all over. I walked over to the driver's side to let him get a look at me — and to let me get a look at him.

He was a young Indian, traditional-style, with long braids hanging down below a beat-up Stetson. "Hi," I said with a grin. "Thanks for stopping."

He didn't return the grin as he gave me a narrow-eyed once-over. "That your truck back there?"

I nodded. " 'Fraid so."

"What's the matter with it?"

"Out of gas."

The corners of the Indian's mouth twitched a little. "Pretty stupid for a white man."

"Yeah? Well, I'm a direct descendant of General Custer. Now we've got my IQ figured out, do I get a ride or don't I?"

He eyed me for a bit. "If I let you in here, are you going to pull a knife on me and steal my truck?"

I let my gaze run over the rust-encrusted outline of the Ford. "*This* truck? I ain't *that* stupid."

He thought some more. "You steal the other truck?"

"No." I felt the edges of my temper start to fray a little. "You know somethin'? You got a real attitude."

The Indian smiled. "Yeah. I've also got a truck with real gas in it." He reached over and opened the door. "Okay, you want a ride, get in."

I pushed a pile of books and papers out of the way and slid in, laying my wet clothes on the seat beside me.

The Indian raised an eyebrow. "You always travel with your laundry?"

I shrugged. "Nope. It just seemed like a good day for a swim."

Two

We rolled along the highway in silence for a while, the old truck gaining speed on the long downgrade north of Cochrane. The Indian braked as the Ford tried to shake itself to pieces on the speed bumps before the intersection at the bottom of the hill. He shot a glance in my direction. "I'm Jesse Firelight. You got a first name, Mr. Custer?"

"Steve." I tried hard not to smile.

"Where are you headed, Steve?"

I shrugged. "Down the road. Where you goin'?"

"Calgary for now."

"That'll do."

Jesse looked puzzled. "What about your truck? You're going back for it, aren't you?"

I shook my head. "The guy I borrowed it from will come and get it. I'm in kind of a hurry to get to the city."

Jesse turned and stared at me so long I thought he was going to rear-end the Lincoln in front of us. "I'll bet you are." He turned back and eased up on the gas just in time to avoid impact.

I sighed. The only way to correct this guy's suspicion that I was a truck thief was to tell him the truth, which would take till about Toronto to tell and we were only going as far as Calgary. That is, I *thought* we were going to Calgary — until Jesse flicked on the signal light and wheeled off the highway and into the business district. "Hey." I was trying to sound unconcerned while scanning both sides of the street for cop stations. "I thought you were goin' to Calgary."

"I am," he said, pulling into a service station. "But unlike the white man, I can read omens." He nodded toward the gas gage. "When I see the red needle starting to close-dance with the big E, I stop and put gas in the tank."

As I gave him a pained look, I caught sight of a pay phone outside the service station. "I need to make a phone call. You gonna wait for me?"

The Indian shrugged. "I might. You need me to lend you a quarter so you can call all your friends?"

"You might be overestimating my number of friends." I slammed the door.

I went inside the phone booth, picked up the receiver, and just stood there. I didn't want to do this. I'd said good-bye once. Talking to anybody back there again was going to tear open a wound a lot deeper than the one in my arm.

I dug out a quarter, dropped it into the slot, and dialed Pop's number. On the other end I could hear it ringing and ringing and ringing. Reluctantly, I hung up. I'd known all along there wouldn't be anybody there. Pop and Beau would still be over at the Quarter Circle. I dialed that number. It rang. Once. Twice. Then, somebody picked it up. God, please don't let it be Raine.

"Hello?"

It was Raine. This was going to be about as bad as it could get. I took a deep breath but couldn't get the words to come out. Silence hung on the line.

"Hello? Hello?" There was a pause. "Steve? Steve, is that you? Where are you? Are you all right? Steve, answer me!"

"Hi, Raine," I managed at last.

"Steve, where are you?"

"It's better you don't know. I won't be here long anyway. Are you alone?"

"Yeah, I'm alone here in the office but there's a couple of detectives outside talking to Mom and your dad."

"Did they hear the phone?"

"No, I'd just come into the arena to feed the horses when it rang. No one else heard it."

"Good. Look, Raine, as soon as they're gone tell Pop the truck's parked along the highway just north of Cochrane. Keys are under the seat. Oh, yeah, and tell him if he wants to drive it home he'd better bring some gas."

There was a long pause. "You mean you actually managed to run out of gas less than an hour from home?"

"Yeah, that's what I mean."

Raine started to laugh. "Steve, you're the dumbest excuse for an outlaw I ever met."

"Yeah, and I guess livin' there in Fenton at the crossroads of the world you've met 'em all." I was hoping to keep her laughing.

It didn't work. Her voice turned serious again. "What're you gonna do now, Steve?"

"I'm okay. I've got a ride. I'll be long gone before the cops get this far."

Another silence. "Gotta go now, Raine," I said softly.

"Please don't go, Steve." Her voice broke into a sob.

"Don't, Raine," I stopped her. My voice went kind of hollow on me. I heard her swallow hard. "Take care of my kid brother, huh. See ya, rich girl."

It worked. "Don't you call me that, you — you sleazy

punk!" The old fire was back in her voice.

That was better. I smiled and gently hung up.

Jesse was waiting outside, engine idling. I got in. He started to drive out onto the street, then paused. "Sure you don't want to go back for the truck?"

I stared out the window into the darkness. "Yeah, I'm sure. I just want to get out of here."

Without another word he pulled back onto the highway and headed for Calgary. Neither of us said anything for a few miles. We were coming into Calgary when I noticed he was looking me over again. Finally, he got to my riding boots. "You a cowboy or are the boots just for show?"

"I've ridden a few horses. Chased a few cows."

He laughed. "*Chased* a few cows. There's a lot more to being a real cowboy than just *chasing* cows."

"Yeah? Well the ones I was acquainted with spent their spare time gettin' into the hayfield and I spent my spare time chasin' them out and fixin' the fence."

"So you *have* done some ranch work?"

I shrugged. "Yeah, for a few weeks once."

"You looking for a job now?"

I shrugged again. "Not really. Mostly I'm just lookin'."

"That figures," the Indian said coolly. "You don't look like the working type. Where do you want out in Calgary?"

I'd already asked myself that question and hadn't come up with a real good answer. "Anywhere the action is."

Jessie threw me a kind of disgusted glance, but didn't say anything. We drove on in silence until he pulled over and stopped at the end of a long, neon-lit strip. "Electric Avenue," he announced with a scornful twist of his lip. "Action enough for you, city boy?"

"It'll do," I said, turning the door handle, which fell

off in my hand. Jesse calmly reached over, took the handle, and screwed it back on. I got out. "Thanks for the ride."

"The pleasure of your company made it all worthwhile," he said, straight-faced. "If you change your mind about a job, The Double C down south where I work might need some help by spring." He gave me one last cool, appraising look and added, "They aren't too fussy about who they hire."

I returned the look and nodded. "Yeah, I can see that."

Jesse laughed, waved, spun a U'y and rattled back the way we'd come. I caught myself half wishing I was going with him. To tell the truth, I wasn't so sure I was up to Electric Avenue tonight. But the fact was, I was here. I started walking, looking at the names of the clubs and bars that lit up the neon signs — Moonshiner's, Coconut Joe's, Buster's, Sharks.

The list went on until all the names started running together and I couldn't remember which was which. There'd been a time I'd have hit every one of them in one night. But this wasn't the night. Right now I was just tired and hungry, and all I wanted was a place to sit down. I picked the first spot that looked like it had good, solid food, walked in and ordered a steak.

I was finished eating and was working on my third cup of coffee before I started thinking about anything but food. Like where I was going to spend the night.

Through a doorway a bar rocked to the sound of loud music and louder laughter. I thought about going in and working on some major forgetting. But somehow the idea of getting bombed out of my mind just didn't cut it anymore. Funny how things change. Or, maybe it's people that change. When I was too young to drink legal I'd try anything to get into a bar, and getting drunk was so cool. Now it just seemed stupid. I shook my head. I really was losin' it. Here I was, nineteen years old and I'd already given up the dope. Now it was the booze. I stared at the glowing end of my cigarette. Yeah, and another month of hanging around the Quarter Circle and Raine would have had me nagged out of that habit, too.

I stood up and crushed out the cigarette. It had been some kind of a day. Up before five and working horses steady all day — until Romero showed up and shot up the party and I ended up on the run again. Now here I was back in the city. Back in the fast lane, where I belonged. Or at least where I *used to* belong. Because, the one thing I wanted to do right now was just go home. Home? I thought with a bitter laugh. Give me a break, Steve. You don't know even what the word means. You were the one grown up enough to run away at twelve. Seven years on the wrong side of Vancouver on your own and it only takes two months at Pop's to make you go all milk and cookies?

No, home was one place I wouldn't be going tonight. But, I had to go somewhere. I paid the bill and left a five-dollar tip for the tired-looking redhead waiting tables. I guess I'll never get over having a soft spot for waitresses. Tracey was a waitress.

I walked out into the cool night air and into a street full of noisy, laughing people. The street was Saturday-night crowded, so crowded I kept bumping into people — yet I'd never felt so alone in my life.

For a long time, I just walked aimlessly. Vaguely, I noticed that the streets were changing. The rowdy but fairly respectable clubs of Electric Avenue were gone. Now the places were older, more run-down, their neon signs more likely to be missing a letter or two. The sidewalks weren't as crowded, and the people on them were different, too. These weren't the loud and happy partyers I'd met earlier. These had the haunted look of people escaping the pain of reality in a bottle.

I caught the movement in the alley out of the corner of

my eye and swung around, cursing myself for being forty kinds of a fool. You walk the streets like this after midnight, you better walk like a cat, every nerve raw and ready for instant fight or flight. I'd been around the block enough times to know the rules. But, I'd let myself get buried in the past and gone wandering along here like some green kid that just fell off the turnip truck. And now it was going to cost me. Just how much depended on what I did in the next few seconds.

All that flashed through my mind in the time it took to dodge the length of pipe that was meant to split my skull. But I was too late to dodge it completely. It caught me a glancing blow on the side of my head and then bounced off my shoulder. Dazed, I went down on one knee, dimly noting that there were four shapes milling around me there in the shadows. Wimps, I thought, disgusted. Back in Vancouver it never took more than two of us to mug somebody.

There were so many of these guys they were getting in each other's way. Before any of them had a chance to hit me again I threw myself at the nearest pair of knees and sent the guy sprawling onto the sidewalk. Back on my feet again, a rush of adrenalin cleared my head and a wave of red-hot anger rushed in behind it. Okay, punks, you want my money, you gotta earn it — in blood. I smashed an elbow into the shortest one's jaw and spun to kick the pipe out of another's hand before he could swing at me again. Three down, a little scorekeeper in the back of my mind whispered gleefully. These guys really weren't good at their work . . .

That's when I took a step backward and tripped over the fourth guy. Mistake number two, Steve, I thought, swearing as I went down. I managed to grab a handful of the guy's jacket and drag him down with me. We wrestled and I'd just managed to get an arm loose and deliver a left to his nose when one of the others grabbed my hair from behind and jerked me down on my back. Before I could roll free the one with the bloody nose let out a screech and launched himself into me like a fighting cat. He landed on me with all his weight — which shouldn't have mattered much since he was such a scrawny little devil. But one of his bony knees landed on my arm, dead center in the same spot the bullet had hit. Pain exploded through my arm and the streetlights went dim.

I wasn't out long. A couple of punches in the face woke me up fast, but even though my mind was up and running again my body totally refused to move. With the two biggest guys kneeling on me there weren't a whole lot of moves I could make anyway. So I just lay there listening to their voices, which seemed to come from a long way off.

"Grab his wallet!"

"Yeah, I got it. Hey, this dude's got some cash."

"How much?"

"I'm countin'. I'm countin'. Seventy-eight bucks!"

"All right! Any cards?"

"Naw, just a driver's license and a picture of a blonde."

"Yeah? Let's see her. Hey, she's not bad."

Shut up, punk, I thought fiercely. You make one crack about her and I swear I'll kill you. How I was going to do it at that exact moment was another question but I would have tried. Then another voice spoke up. "Hurry up! Let's split before somebody comes along. Ditch the wallet, stupid. You get caught with it on you and you're in big trouble. Okay, let's go."

A weight lifted off my chest and breathing got a lot easier as the two who had been holding me down stood up. Then, somebody landed a kick in my stomach. "That's for what you did to my nose," a voice snuffled. It didn't do much damage since he was wearing running shoes, and I was real pleased about his nose.

I heard the sound of running feet on the sidewalk. Then, silence, peaceful silence.

The next thing I heard was the sound of sirens. The thin wail stabbed through my foggy brain like a sharp knife. I staggered to my feet, dizzy and half-sick but feeling the adrenalin rushing through me again. Sirens meant cops. I had to get out of there.

I started walking, a little unsteadily at first, but as the dizziness eased off, I broke into a run. By the time the sirens turned the corner I was down an alley and out of sight.

I don't know how long I ran. Didn't know where I was running to — just what I was running from. Putting distance between me and the sound of sirens the way a deer runs from the sound of wolves on its trail.

The only sounds now were my own breathing and the pounding of my heart, so loud they drowned out the steady hum of city traffic. I slowed to a walk, stumbled, and almost fell. But I caught myself and stood leaning against the side of a building, trying to figure out where I was. Downtown somewhere. Right downtown. Where the big-time businessmen hang out. Glass and concrete buildings towered cold and soulless on all sides but the streets were empty. The power brokers had all gone home for the night. I shivered, partly because of the sweat cooling on my body, but mostly from the haunted feeling of the empty high-rises. I decided I'd rather be back on the mean streets of drunks and muggers. At least those places had a heart — even if it was an evil one.

Then, just a block or two ahead, I caught sight of some trees. A green oasis in a concrete desert. A place to hide out for a while. I started toward it. As I pushed myself away from the side of the building I noticed that a smear of red stayed behind. But it didn't seem to matter much right then.

The park wasn't very big. Just some grass, a few dead flowers, a couple of rows of spruce trees, and a little fountain in the middle. But it was quiet and empty and that was good enough. I picked the biggest spruce and crawled in under the low-hanging branches. The ground was deep-carpeted with fallen needles and it smelled like Christmas. I'd slept in worse places and right now I should be tired enough to sleep in the middle of a train track. But, as I leaned back against the tree trunk and closed my eyes, sleep didn't come easy. It never did.

There would be the ghosts to deal with first. All the mistakes I'd made, all the dumb things I'd done to mess up my life. They always came around to haunt me for a while before I slept. They'd been coming a long time now and they didn't scare me much. I was tougher than they were.

But Tracey was a different story. She'd been gone for over three months now, but every time I closed my eyes her face was so real I was sure I could reach out and touch her. God, how long does it take to forget? How long before it quits hurting?

But, deep down, I didn't want to forget Tracey. Not ever. She was the best thing that ever happened to me. The one person I wanted to stay with forever. And now she was dead.

I shifted my weight, trying to get comfortable, and pain knifed through my arm. I could feel warm blood trickling down my arm, dripping off my fingertips. I forced myself to sit up, pull off Pop's jacket, and retie Raine's scarf as tight as I could. It was too dark to see how the wound looked, which was just as well. I put Pop's jacket back on, laid my head on my own damp jacket, and crashed.

Three

*J*ust like Sleeping Beauty, I got woke up by a kiss. Mine came from a cold, black nose and a long, pink tongue that belonged to someone who had recently downed a lot of Dr. Ballard's. I opened my eyes to find myself eyeball-to-eyeball with a big black-and-tan German shepherd who was licking my face, whining, and looking so worried his eyebrows were crooked.

"Hey," I muttered, struggling to escape, "knock it off, dog! I ain't dead. Not quite. But one more faceful of your breath could definitely push me over."

I heard a man's voice on the other side of the row of trees. Just what I needed. Company. Like a grouse in the deep woods I froze — and hoped I was invisible there in the shadows.

The voice was getting closer and sounded out of breath. I could hear running footsteps, too. "Triscuit! Come back here, Triscuit!" The dog pricked up his ears and stared in the direction of the voice. So did I. Sure enough, through a gap in the trees I spotted him. A genuine jogger. Cute little baby-blue sweatsuit and all.

"Tri-i-i-scuit!" The dog whined softly, looked guiltily toward the jogger and then worriedly back at me. I gave his ears a scratch. "Hey, dog," I whispered, "you think *I've* got problems? At least my name ain't Triscuit."

The dog gave what sounded like an embarrassed whine and then reached out his pink tongue to wash a streak of dried blood off my hand. I wasn't so sure I liked the way his eyes lit up at the taste of it. "Time to go, Triscuit. Your yuppie's callin'."

"Triscuit?" The voice was taking on a desperate tone. "Where are you, Triscuit? If you're nosing around in something dead and disgusting again . . ."

I grinned. Only half right, huh Triscuit? Triscuit grinned back, gave my hand one more lick, and trotted back into the upper class.

For a while, I stayed out of sight, listening for more joggers and other city wildlife but the park stayed quiet. It was safe to come out. I crawled stiffly out from under the tree and realized I was about cold enough to grow icicles. I had a headache, a few hundred aching muscles, and generally felt like I was getting the flu — which I guess is how you're supposed to feel after you've been mugged.

My arm had quit bleeding but it was going to need some attention. I gingerly worked the blood-crusted sleeve loose from my skin and spent an interesting ten minutes picking chunks of dirt and grit out of the raw bullet hole. I still couldn't get it very clean so I walked over to where the little stone fountain was shooting jets of water into the sunshine and washed in the ice-cold water. Then I had a good, long drink until it occurred to me that maybe you weren't supposed to drink out of fountains these days. Maybe they ran recycled sewage or something through there. Oh well, it was a little late to worry.

I rebandaged my arm and eased into my still-damp but reasonably clean shirt and jacket. Then I picked up Pop's bloody jacket. Maybe I should wash it. No way. I'd already done more laundry in the last twenty-four hours than in the whole rest of my life put together. I rolled the jacket up and tossed it way back under a tree. With any luck Triscuit would find it and drag it home to Baby Blue. The guy could use a little excitement in his life.

Then I hit the road. I walked through the Sunday-morning peace, working my way out of the cold concrete canyons of downtown and on out through the rundown residential districts. Met a couple of Saturday-night drunks still heading home. Met a couple more dogs. One was a pit bull that sat in the middle of the sidewalk and snarled at me. I snarled back but detoured around him. Let him keep his sidewalk. Met a streetwise, old yellow tomcat sitting on a fence carefully washing a bloodied eartip. He gave me a thoughtful green look and then slowly closed one eye. I laughed and returned the wink. Yeah, cat, I know what you mean. Hang out on the streets at night and you gotta expect to bleed a little.

Gradually, I found myself in an industrial area. It looked the same as the industrial area of every city I've ever seen. Piles of gravel, bins of rusty scrap metal, tangled heaps of old oilfield equipment, corpses of cars piled five-deep at auto wreckers. It sprawled across dusty lots studded with brown, gone-to-seed weeds. Acres and acres of ugly.

I'd been walking for two or three hours now. That, combined with the fact I hadn't eaten today and had done a fair amount of bleeding last night was starting to make me feel kind of light-headed. I had to blink hard once in a while to make the pavement ahead of me quit dissolving into wavy patterns. A couple of times I caught myself staggering. I needed to rest. I spotted a bus stop bench and gratefully sank into it, leaned back, and closed my eyes. The dizziness retreated, leaving me just plain tired. The warm sun felt good on my face and my aching muscles started to relax. Gradually the hum of the traffic seemed to fade into the distance . . .

A hand touched my shoulder and I jumped like I'd been burned. Where was I? And who was the big guy in a uniform looking down at me? Oh God, not a cop! My heart missed a beat and then started pounding so hard it almost drowned out the man's worried voice. "Are you all right, son?" I took a deep breath and tried to act normal. Not wanting him to see the panic in my eyes, I focused on the words on his uniform. Calgary Transit System. I went weak with relief. You're really losin' it, Steve; spooked by a bus driver. "Yeah, sure, I'm okay."

"Sure you're not sick?"

I shook my head. "Just tired. What time is it?"

He checked his watch. "One-fifteen."

Great. I must have slept for nearly an hour on a bus bench in the middle of Calgary. That's a real intelligent way to stay out of sight. Keep this up, Steve, and you're gonna wind up dead.

The bus driver climbed back on his bus. "Well, get on," he said impatiently. "I've got a route to cover."

I gave him a blank look. "Oh, I wasn't waitin' for the bus," I said.

"Punk," the driver muttered as he closed the door. An old lady stared down at me through a window like I was a piece of toxic trash. The bus moved away. I got up and started walking.

Just ahead there was a fairly major-looking north-south road. That should take me out of town. I'd had all the city I could handle for a while.

I walked another hour or more not daring to try thumbing a ride in the city in case I attracted a cop. At last I passed the city limits sign. I started walking backwards with my thumb out, but the cars just kept on swishing past. With my battered face, uncombed hair, and wrinkled clothes, I wouldn't pick me up either. I gave up thumbing and just walked on.

After a couple of miles I glanced back and spotted a truck with a horse trailer coming. Maybe a rodeo cowboy going down the road. Cowboys didn't scare off too easy. I stuck out my thumb. As the truck started to slow, I grinned — and then caught a glimpse of a car coming over the hill behind the truck. It was sleek, black, and low. Romero's black Jag! I spun around, jumped into the ditch, and, in seconds, was out of sight behind a hedge of poplars. Through an opening in the branches I watched the car pull out and pass the truck and trailer. As it came back into the right lane I got a good look at it. It was a BMW with a gray-haired woman behind the wheel. I swore out loud. How did I ever get so spooked I was jumping at shadows? But then the wound in my arm gave a throb and I *knew* how. Somebody shoots you, you start taking them real serious.

Before I could get back through the trees the truck and trailer were pulling away. I wondered what that cowboy was saying to himself about now — but I didn't really want to know.

I jammed my hands deep into my jacket pockets, hunched my shoulders against the wind, and started walking again. My mind slid back to the first time I'd walked away. When I was twelve and decided that life on the road couldn't be as tough as it was at home. I'd found out real fast I was wrong about that. But not fast enough. By then I'd made my choice. I wondered how different things might be now if I'd been more like my kid brother, Beau. Stuck things out at home. Just kept plodding along, staying out of trouble. One thing for sure, I wouldn't be in this mess now. But then I wouldn't have met Tracey. Wouldn't have lost Tracey . . .

There was a sudden blast of an air horn right behind me. I jumped. Somehow, I had daydreamed myself right off the shoulder onto the highway. The truck, an empty cattle liner, whistled by so close I could have touched it. The driver was shaking his fist at me. Normally, I'd have given him a little sign language of my own but right now I was just too tired to care. I kept on walking. Then I saw the liner's brake lights come on and heard the whoosh of the air brakes. Next thing the truck was backing up toward me. I sighed. With my luck I'd run into some psycho truck driver who took walking in the middle of the road so personal he was coming back to run over me. I leapt into the dry roadside grass. If he wanted me he'd have to ditch the rig to get me.

The big red cab slid to a stop beside me. QUILLER CATTLE, the sign on the door said. The door swung open and a big, beefy guy whose face seemed to have frozen into a permanent scowl glared down at me. "Well, don't just stand there gawkin'. You need a ride bad enough to stand in the middle of the road obstructing traffic, get in. I ain't got all day to sit here burnin' diesel while you think about it."

I stared at him. I'd been talked to nicer by people who were about to try to kill me. But, a ride was a ride. I sauntered over to the passenger side and climbed in. The big guy wheeled the rig back into the driving lane and fed her some diesel before glancing in my direction. "Where you headed?" he barked.

"South."

"Yeah? I gathered that from the direction you were walkin'. *Where* south?"

I shrugged. "However far the ride's goin'."

"That'll be Nanton."

"Where's that?"

"Couple of towns down the road. That's where I turn off and head west. And it's about far enough from home to make sure Rachel don't see me with you in the truck."

This conversation wasn't making a whole lot of sense. "Who's Rachel?" I asked.

The driver sighed. "My wife. Every time she catches me pickin' up a hitchhiker I get the lecture. 'You never know. Could be another Charles Ng,' she says. Figures one of these days I'm gonna wind up dead in a ditch while some serial killer drives off inconspicuously in my little old cattle liner." He dropped the truck a gear as we started up a hill and then glanced sideways at my bruised face. "Come to think of it," he muttered, "in your case she could be right."

"So," I said tiredly, "if I look so dangerous, why'd you stop for me?"

The driver readjusted his bulk in the seat and took his time answering. "Looks can be deceiving. I remember bein' your age. Back in the sixties. Those were the days. I hitchhiked all over the country. Had hair halfway to my waist. Guess you'd never believe it now." A grin fought its way through the scowl on his face as he lifted his greasy cap off a shiny bald head. "Yep, made it all the way to Woodstock." His voice trailed off and got lost somewhere back in his rock-and-roll days.

"No kiddin'." I tried hard to picture this good ol' red-neck truck driver as a sixties flower child. "That where you met Rachel?"

He laughed softly. "Rachel was never *that* young."

I just let that one go by. We drove on, the roar of the big engine loud in the silence between us. Then, all of a sudden, he looked in my direction again. "Name's Tom Quiller."

I hesitated. Too long. "Steve," I said.

I could feel the easiness that had been building up between us melt away as Tom shot me a nervous look. I wondered if he was imagining me wheeling his cattle liner into some faraway city while his bones bleached in the prairie wind. The miles clicked off under the truck's big wheels. We rolled on through a couple of little prairie towns. When we hit the third town Tom broke the silence. "Nanton," he said.

I didn't say anything. He turned on his signal light and the air brakes sighed as he pulled into the turning lane. "This is where I go west," he said. The wind whipped a cloud of dust across the road. A stream of warm air from the heater was blowing across my knees, the seat was getting to feel real comfortable, and even the country music bleating from the radio was beginning to sound kind of friendly. A lot friendlier than it looked outside. I let the silence drag out until Tom gave me a sharp glance. "West might be just as good as south," I said.

He sighed and shifted gear. "How'd I know you were gonna say that?" he muttered.

I just sat tight and gave him a grin as we crawled around the corner and headed west. Tom worked his way back up through the gears. "Well," he said grudgingly, "guess you can ride to my turnoff. But then you're on your own. I sure ain't about to adopt you."

I returned his scowl. "I hope not. Baldness could be contagious." The corner of a grin almost escaped him before he got his face under control again.

A few more miles slid by as I stared out at the bare fields. It looked like I was going to be sleeping under the stars again tonight. I could handle that. There were worse places to spend the night than under a tree. If there were any trees in this country. The way it looked around here I might be sleeping in the shade of a sow thistle.

But, as we went farther west the land began to fold itself into foothills. The big, unfenced grainfields were changing into hayfields and pastures dotted with grazing cattle. Once in a while a long lane led to a cluster of buildings surrounded by corral fences. And, I noted with relief, there was even an occasional patch of trees. Ranch country. I read the signs on the big wooden gates. Rushing Creek Ranches, The Rocking R, Elk Valley Ranch, The Double C . . .

I sat bolt upright and took a second look over my shoulder to make sure I'd read right. "Hey!" I yelled, "Stop, Tom!"

Tom jumped like he'd been shot and hit the brakes so hard he almost jack-knifed the trailer. He wrestled the rig under control, pulled over on the shoulder, and turned to glare at me. "What the — "

"Sorry," I said, reaching for the door handle. "I didn't mean it had to be quite that sudden but this is where I get off."

"Somethin' special about right here?" Tom warily surveyed the shadowy weed-filled ditches like he expected this might be where I'd picked to dump his body before I lit out for Mexico with the truck.

"No, not here." I grinned. "Back there. Thanks for the ride, Tom. Say hi to Rachel." As I jumped out of the truck I caught one final glimpse of Tom. He was shaking his head.

He pulled away in a cloud of diesel smoke. Ol' Tom was an okay guy. I raised two fingers in a v-shaped salute. "Peace, man," I yelled above the rumble of the engine. Then I turned and walked back toward the Double C, hoping real hard this was the same Double C I thought it was.

At the gateway I stopped and studied the sign. Two big, red C's overlapped above a cartoon drawing of a couple of fierce, fire-breathing long-horned cows. In smaller red letters it said, CRAZY COW RANCH. Whoever owned this place had a sense of humor. Well, they'd need it if this was where Jesse Firelight worked.

I trudged up the long, narrow lane that wound between two rows of tall trees. Spruce trees. If worse came to worst, at least I knew where I was sleeping tonight.

Four

---

*T*hen I was on top of a hill looking down at the ranch spread out below me. Big, weathered old log house, red barn, a lot of corrals and outbuildings spread around. It looked like a ranch should look. But before I had time to take in any more details about the layout something else caught my eye. Dead ahead, in front on an open-doored Quonset, sat the worst-looking, rust-eaten old Ford half-ton I'd ever seen in my life — except once. Yesterday, to be exact, when it had pulled up to give me a ride. This *was* the right Double C.

A pair of feet were sticking out from under the truck. They seemed to be attached to somebody who was doing a lot of muttering and clanging somewhere in the vicinity of the universal joint. I strolled on over and gave the nearest foot a little nudge with my toe. A surprised grunt came from under the truck and the rest of the body came wriggling out to join the feet. Sure enough, Jesse Firelight, in person.

"Hi," I said. "Remember me?"

Jesse reached up and brushed a strand of long, black

hair out of his eyes, leaving an arc of grease across his cheekbone. With the braids and all it had kind of a warpaint effect. I liked it.

"You're the kind that's hard to forget," he said in a tone that pretty well eliminated any chance he meant it as a compliment.

I let that go by and nodded to the decaying Ford. "Told you that thing wasn't worth stealin'."

For a minute, Jesse didn't say a word. His eyes did a slow tour of me from head to foot, hesitating for a thorough inspection of the bruises on my face. "That truck looks considerably healthier than you do. What happened? You meet somebody who took a dislike to your charming personality?"

"No, I met some degenerate low-lifes who took a liking to my money."

Jesse raised his eyebrows. "Even more degenerate than you?"

"Probably not. But there were more of them." Before he could ask another stupid question I moved the conversation back to the truck. "So, what's wrong with it?"

Jesse shrugged. "If I knew that I would fix it and become independently wealthy like the mechanics in town who live off the proceeds of my misfortune." Then, totally deadpan, he added, "I am a hunter of the buffalo, a rider of the plains. I am not into the intestines of the iron horse."

I just stared at him, waiting for him to laugh. He didn't. "Well, get out of the way and let me have a look," I said, sliding under the dusty truck. "Hand me that flashlight."

"With pleasure."

One look was all it took to see that Jesse's universal joint was even worse off than the rest of his truck. I crawled out, handed Jesse the light, and wiped my hands on my jeans.

Jesse gave me a questioning look. "Well?"

"Nothin' spectacular. Just needs a new U-joint."

Jesse groaned. "Not another garage bill."

"You don't need to take it to a garage. Any fool can put in a U-joint."

Jesse eyed me thoughtfully. "So, I guess that means you could do it, huh?"

I ignored the insult. "Could don't mean will."

Jesse's eyes appraised me a while longer. "But you might if it meant getting a free meal and a place to sleep tonight."

"A free meal. You checked mechanics' rates lately?"

"You checked the price of a ten-ounce T-bone lately?"

I was just about to tell Jesse I wasn't all that hungry when my stomach growled so loud I was sure the old, gray-whiskered collie sleeping in the Quonset would wake up and want to fight. But the dog missed his chance.

Jesse didn't miss a thing. He smiled a slow, triumphant smile. "Deal," he said. "Come on up to the house and we'll get them to throw in an extra potato."

"Potato? What happened to the steak?" Jesse just laughed and kept walking.

Outside the back door he stopped and turned to face me. "So, I guess your name isn't really Custer, huh, Steve?"

I met his eyes. "I guess not," I said, trying to think fast. In all the years I'd been away from home I'd been in and out of trouble most of the time — but never bad enough trouble to use anything but my real name. Now, though, with not anywhere close to enough distance between me and that run-in with Romero, there was no way I could be Steve Garrett. I tried to think of a name that sounded reasonable but the only thing that came into my head was Billy the Kid, the nickname Beau had hung on me back when we were little. I looked Jesse right in the eye and said, "Bonney. Steve Bonney."

Jesse took that in and nodded solemnly. "Same last name as Billy the Kid, huh?"

"Yeah, Pop figures we might be related way back."

Jesse nodded again. "Billy the Kid and General Custer, too."

I shrugged. "Yeah, well, it was a big family."

Right then the door opened, spilling a big pool of light, warmth, and the smell of something cooking out into the darkness.

"Well, Jesse! I thought you'd forgotten to show up to eat. But I should have known better than that." I looked up to see a big, gray-haired woman in faded jeans, riding boots, and an apron. The woman spotted me. "And I see you've brought in another stray. He follow you home like that big hairy dog you brought home last week?"

Jesse laughed. "More or less, Connie. This is Steve . . ." I caught the pause and the little twitch at the corner of his mouth. ". . . Bonney. Figures he's a mechanic so I, uh, kind of promised him a steak if he'd fix my U-joint."

"Oh, you kinda did, did you? Mighty generous with my steaks, aren't you?" the woman said with a grin that made me think that if Jesse had given away a whole cow she'd let him get away with it. She shifted her gaze to me. "Well, come on in, Steve. If Jesse's gone and made himself a deal we'll just have to honor it." She held out a floury hand, laughed, wiped it on her apron, and tried again. "Biscuits," she explained, shaking hands with a grip that meant business. "I'm Connie Johanneson. Carl," she called over her shoulder, "we've got company." A man came around the corner. He was also big, gray, and wearing an apron.

Connie introduced Carl and me and then added, "Jesse's swindled this poor boy into fixing that decrepit truck of his in return for a steak dinner."

Carl grinned and held out a big, calloused hand. "Sounds fair enough to me. Too bad we're having stew tonight."

"Oh, that's all right," Jesse put in cheerfully. "Steve won't mind."

I didn't have a chance to express an opinion on that because Connie cut in. "You've got that right, Jesse," she said, straight-faced as she opened the fridge and came out with a steak about the size of a dinner plate, "because Steve will be eating steak, just like you promised. But don't go getting *your* hopes up, Jess," she added with a wink in my direction. "*You* still get stew."

I could tell Connie and me were going to get along just fine.

During supper I mainly kept my mouth shut — except when I was stuffing it with steak — and learned a lot about the Johannesons. Like the fact that finding Carl in the kitchen with Connie was no more unlikely than finding Connie out working cattle with Carl. That's how they'd been doing things for forty years now, together. They'd built up a herd of two or three hundred prime cows from a handful of scrubs that were so wild a neighbor practically gave them away, just to get rid of them. That's how the Double C had got its double meaning, Carl and Connie and Crazy Cow.

Most of the time Carl and Connie did all the work themselves, except for maybe hiring a haying crew. But now they were getting older and they'd hired Jesse full-time — adopted him probably would have been closer. I figured he had to be about the best-treated ranch hand in Alberta. But then again, it seemed like treating people good came naturally to the Johannesons. They seemed to think that having a dirty, beat-up stranger drop in out of nowhere for supper was no more unusual than having the kid next door stop in. They never asked me a single question all the time we were eating. Well, that's not quite true. Connie *did* want to know if I could eat another piece of pie.

After supper I went to the bunkhouse with Jesse. It wasn't fancy but it was considerably more comfortable than your average spruce tree. Jesse pointed to a spare, made-up bunk, said, "Help yourself," and then seemed to totally forget I was even there. He sat down at the table under the light and dragged a big pile of books over in front of him. I recognized some of the books. They were the same ones I'd shared a truck seat with yesterday — and they definitely weren't my idea of a fun way to spend an evening.

It didn't really look like Jesse was having much fun either. I sat on the bunk and watched as he leafed through a couple of books, scribbled something on a piece of paper, muttered, crumpled up the paper, and heaved it in the general direction of the garbage can. Then he started all over again.

After about half an hour of instant replays I was about to fall asleep sitting up. I took off my boots, lay down and pulled the blankets over me. *That* got Jesse's attention. He turned around and stared at me, then glanced at the clock, and back to me again. "You wild and crazy city boys always go to bed at eight-thirty?"

I forced my eyes to stay open. "Yeah." I yawned. "If the company's too boring."

"You always sleep in your clothes, too?"

I yawned again. "Cold out here in the country." I didn't bother to add, "Plus I've got a bullet hole in my arm I don't want to use for show and tell right now."

I eased into a more comfortable position, closed my eyes, and, for once, was out like a light.

The next thing I knew Jesse was shaking me awake. It was still dark out. "Rise and shine, city boy. My chariot awaits medical attention and you've already eaten your share of the bargain."

I groaned and rolled over. "Shoot that thing between the headlights and put it out of its misery."

Jesse jerked all the blankets off me. "Do us both a favor. Go take a shower." Not awake enough to fight back, I stumbled off to the bathroom.

My eyes were open by the time I staggered onto dry land again. I was just about to put my dirty clothes back on when the door opened far enough for Jesse to dump a pile of clean ones at my feet. "For a guy who only two days ago was drying his laundry, you sure get dirty. You can wear these long enough to wash yours." I tried to decide if I should be grateful or insulted. One thing for sure, I was sick of wearing everybody else's clothes. But at least these came a lot closer to fitting than either Beau's or Pop's ever had.

We had breakfast with Carl and Connie and then I got seriously acquainted with the underside of Jesse's Ford. It took a fair amount of cussing and knuckle-skinning but I finally got the old U-joint tore out of there. Wearily, I crawled out into the daylight. Jesse looked me up and down. "Now you've gone and got *my* clothes dirty," he said disgustedly. I gently but firmly placed the grease-covered U-joint in Jesse's nice, clean hand. "Take that to town and get another one just like it."

He eyed it like it might bite. "Hey, that's part of *your* job."

"Uh-uh, I said I'd fix it. I didn't say I'd get the parts."

Jesse sighed and gingerly set the part in the back of the farm truck Carl had let him borrow. "Well," he said as he climbed in, "don't you at least want to come along for the ride and take in the local color?"

"Nope," I said, pulling up a convenient bale of hay and sitting down for an in-depth visit with the old dog.

Jesse gave me a long, puzzled look and drove away, shaking his head.

He was gone for quite a while. Exactly how long I wasn't sure. The dog and I ran out of things to talk about and both of us took a nap. By the time I woke up again my stomach and the height of the sun in the sky agreed it must be close to noon. I was beginning to wonder if I dared show up at the house for another meal when Jesse finally drove in. He didn't look happy when he got out of the truck — empty-handed. "Well, where's the part?" I asked. "You do remember what I sent you after?"

Jesse glowered at me. "They didn't have one in town. Or in the next two towns up the highway. I finally had to order one."

"Well, obviously you were lookin' in all the wrong places."

"Yeah? Well, city boy, where would *you* have looked for one?"

I raised an eyebrow at the rising hulk of Jesse's truck. "How about a junkyard?"

Fortunately, just then Connie came out on the step and called us for dinner.

We were nearly done eating when Jesse got around to mentioning that the new U-joint wouldn't be in for a couple of days. Well, that about finished that. Deal or no deal, there was no way I could hang around here that long. Besides, fixing the U-joint was supposed to be worth one steak. At the rate I was putting away the grub here I'd end up having to build a whole new truck.

Right after dinner I thanked Connie for the meals, collected the clothes she'd washed for me, and said goodbye to her and Carl. Then I changed back into my own clothes and hunted up Jesse. "Here," I said, handing him back his clothes. "Thanks for the loan. See you around some day."

Jesse looked up from the book he was reading. "You can't go yet."

"Yeah, Jesse, I can." I reached for the doorknob.

Jesse stood up. "But what about my truck?"

I shrugged. "Sorry, Jess. The deal didn't include hangin' around here forever."

I was halfway out the door when Jesse's mocking voice stopped me in my tracks. "What's the matter, city boy, can you see the dust from the sheriff's posse on the horizon?"

I swung around to face him. "What's that supposed — "

"Steve!" Carl's voice boomed from outside. "I'm glad I caught you before you left. I've got something to ask you."

My eyes unlocked from Jesse's. I took a couple of deep breaths and turned to meet Carl. If Carl had caught the tension in that moment he didn't let on. He just grinned and rubbed the stubble on his chin.

"Connie and I've been talkin'. Well, mainly Connie's been talkin' and I've been listenin'. But, I think she might be right. Maybe we could use another hand here for the winter and on through calvin' time. And since you and Jesse seem to get along so good . . . Well, how about it, Steve, can you use the work?"

Five

Stay here? Just a couple hundred miles from where the cops knew I was two days ago? Just a couple hundred miles from where Romero had tried to kill me? Not likely, Carl. But, for once in my life, I thought before I said anything.

I was flat broke. Winter was breathing down my neck and, without wheels, the only way to get anywhere was walking or hitchhiking, neither of which was exactly the most inconspicuous way to travel. But the Double C was inconspicuous. It was so quiet here you could probably go all winter and never see a stranger. Nobody would ever think I'd end up in a place like this. Carl and Connie didn't have a suspicious bone in them. That left just one wild card — Jesse.

I turned to look at him again, trying to read his eyes. But his face was expressionless, his dark eyes level and steady on mine. Whatever he was thinking was for him to know and me not to find out. I took a deep breath. Any way I looked at it, I was going to have to take my chances. Might as well take them on Jesse

Firelight. I turned back to Carl. "Sure, I could use a job."

Carl grinned. "Don't bite too fast, Steve. You haven't heard the wages yet. Five hundred a month and all you can eat is about as good as we can do over the winter."

I returned the grin. "Considering you don't know how much I can eat, I'd say that sounds fair." Carl laughed and shook my hand so violently I had to grit my teeth to keep from hollering. That arm better quit hurting before I had to start working.

Carl turned to Jesse. "Okay, Jess, you got yourself a partner. Tomorrow you two can head up to the cabin on the lease for a month or so. There's still fair grazing up there but it's time those cows got a little hay as well. You guys can stay up there and babysit them till winter sets in. Right now, you can get Steve a horse — and teach him to ride it if necessary." He grinned in my direction.

Jesse gave me a long, thoughtful look before turning back to Carl. "Yes sir," he said, "and I could probably learn a thing or two from him, too."

Jesse and I sat on the top rail of the horse corral. "Well," he said, "which horse do you want?"

I looked them over. They were a good enough looking bunch of cow horse. Solid quarter horses mostly. But nothing special. Except for one. A tall, hard-muscled strawberry roan gelding. I nodded toward him. "Roan's the best horse there."

Jesse nodded. "Hundred percent on that test, city boy."

"Okay, then, I'll take him."

"No, you won't."

"Why not?"

Jesse didn't answer. Instead he whistled softly. The roan stopped munching hay, glanced in our direction and walked over. Jesse jumped down, dug in his pocket, and came up with a lump of sugar that the horse crunched down. "Because he's mine." Jesse laughed as the roan vacuumed up and down his sleeve for more sugar. "Quit it, Firebird, you miserable crowbait. After what that truck's been costing me I can't afford to take *you* to the dentist."

Firebird. The name fit the horse all right, I thought, taking in the way his red and white flecked body gradually darkened to pure, fire-red head, legs, mane and tail. I climbed down for a closer look. "I suppose you named him from some old Indian legend, huh?"

Jesse shook his head. "Not exactly. I named him after the kind of car I'd be driving if I had money like you city boys."

I sighed and turned back to study the other horses. "Okay." I pointed. "I'll take the black."

"Old Ladysox?"

"The horse and I ain't been formally introduced. If the black one's Old Ladysox, then, yeah, I want her."

"Why?" Jesse was looking at me real weird.

I thought that one over. "Because she's black."

"So?"

"So, two of the best horses I ever rode were black."

Jesse shrugged as if there was no point in even arguing with anybody so obviously dumb. "She won't like you."

I gave him a dirty look. "Sure she will. Everybody likes me."

At that point Jesse had a coughing fit. But he handed me a halter. "Okay, go get your horse."

I took the halter and walked slowly toward the mare. "Whoa, Lady. Easy girl," I said, automatically shortening her name to something halfway sensible. Maybe she did have two high, white socks on her hind legs but Ladysox sounded like the name of a sissy baseball team.

The mare flattened her ears and turned her rear end toward me. Obviously I'd dropped the wrong half of her name. This horse was no lady. In fact, I was getting the feeling that Jesse might have been right. Lady definitely didn't like me. I could feel Jesse's amused eyes on my back as I came up beside her and she neatly swung her hindquarters over to keep her heels aimed in my direction. Okay, horse, that about does it. Either you're gonna kick my teeth in or you're not. But one way or another we're about to find out 'cause you're not gonna bluff your way out of being caught.

I stepped up behind her and gave her a slap on the rump. "Cut it out, Lady," I growled. "Whoa, now." The mare trembled a little at my touch and shot a surprised look at me over her shoulder but she stood still and her ears came up a little. I slipped the halter on and led her over to Jesse. "Okay, now what?"

He gave me a look I couldn't read and nodded. "Tie her up to the fence. We'll go and find a saddle."

We went into the tack room and I picked out a spare saddle that looked about right. I had started outside with it when Jesse asked, "You want me to show you how to put it on?" I glanced back over my shoulder to see if he was kidding but his face was dead serious.

"I'll manage," I said coolly, refusing to rise to the bait.

"Okay, city boy, go ahead. I'll be there as soon as I put this new cinch on my saddle." This time there was a hint of a grin on his face and I wondered why.

I nodded and headed out to the corral. Lady was standing there half-asleep, drooping her lower lip and resting one hind foot. "Whoa, girl," I said automatically, laying the saddle blanket on her back and smoothing out the wrinkles. Then I set the saddle on. The mare sighed like she was tired just thinking about the whole deal. As I reached down for the cinch. I caught a glimpse of Connie coming across the yard.

She waved and hollered something I didn't hear. I waved back. I fastened the front and back cinches and

was just about to pull the front one up tight when Connie
called again, "Steve! Wait!" I wondered what she was
getting all uptight about. I wasn't going anywhere until
Jesse got here. I'd just finish tightening the cinch and
then see what she wanted. I slid my hand under the cinch
ring and smoothed Lady's thick fall hair out of the way.
Then I gave the latigo strap a good hard pull.

And that's when Lady blew her mind. Totally. She gave
a squeal of pure fury, reared back, and hit the end of her
halter rope like a runaway freight train. The rope snapped
like a guitar string and the horse went bucking and kicking across the corral like she'd never had a saddle on in
her life. A few jumps later she must have decided the
saddle wasn't about to come off because she quit bucking and settled into a high-stepping trot, holding her head
and tail in the air and showing off like she figured she'd
just done something downright wonderful.

I was still standing there staring in amazement when
Connie came up beside me. "That is one strange horse," I
said to her and then added, "What'd you want me for,
Connie?"

Connie's face melted into a slow grin. "Actually,
Steve, I came to tell you something about Ladysox. You
always have to untie her before you tighten the cinch or
she gets mad and pulls back — as you may have noticed."

I watched the mare make another circuit of the corral.
"She got any other weird habits?"

"Well, mainly she doesn't seem to like men much at
all. She was broke by a girl who worked here a few years
back. Guess she just grew up thinking women were the
ones to pay attention to." Connie chuckled. "Of course,
you can't really fault her logic, can you?" She went right
on without waiting for an answer to that. "Come to think
of it, I guess I'm the only person around here she hasn't
tried to dump in the last couple of years. Carl and Jesse

avoid her like the plague. You sure you don't want a different horse, Steve?"

I thought that over. Trying to work cattle with a horse just waiting for a chance to do you wrong didn't sound real inviting. On the other hand, sometimes a bad horse was just a good horse in disguise and if you could turn them around and get their respect they'd work their heart out for you.

I caught a glimpse of Jesse, leaning on the fence, watching me with just a hint of a grin twitching the corners of his mouth. Just like the grin he had when he asked me if I wanted him to show me how to saddle Lady. He'd known what was going to happen all along. He'd set me up. No, that wasn't exactly true. He just hadn't stopped me from setting myself up. Okay, round one to Jesse Firelight, with a little help from a horse named Ladysox.

I turned back to Connie. "No," I said, "I don't want to change. Lady and me will get along." I walked over to corner my horse and get started on round two.

Jesse got saddled up, climbed on Firebird, and sat there smiling, waiting for me to get on Lady. Okay, Jesse, smile all you want. This horse is *not* about to unload me. I took a short rein and a deep breath, and swung into the saddle. And . . .

I was absolutely right. Lady *didn't* unload me. I'd like to be able to take some credit for that fact but the truth was she didn't dump me because she didn't even try. As I settled into the saddle she gave one big sigh like I'd just ruined her whole day and then set off down the trail behind Firebird as peaceful as all get-out. Jesse looked back over his shoulder at us — and smiled.

We rode all over the ranch that afternoon and I watched Lady's every move like a hawk. And she just kept right on behaving herself — and watching my every move like a hawk. When we finally got home and unsaddled it was my turn to heave a big sigh. I had a feeling that riding that mare was going to be the hardest work of my life. All she was waiting for was the first time I got careless — and I'm not naturally a careful person.

Six

R ight after breakfast next morning we packed up to head for the grazing lease out west. While Jesse and I saddled the horses Carl and Connie loaded the four-by-four with groceries, blankets, fencing supplies, and whatever else we might need for this little fall vacation. After Jesse finished with Firebird he caught another horse and strapped a pack saddle on him. I couldn't figure that one; all the supplies were in the truck. Jesse caught my puzzled look. "We're going to be fencing in places a truck would never go, city boy. Taking a pack horse beats carrying the posts on your back," he said cheerfully. I didn't ask any questions. I had a feeling that whatever I didn't know about this job I'd find out about all too soon.

We led the horses over to the truck. "All loaded up," Carl announced. Jesse surveyed the piles of stuff in the back. "Not quite," he said, handing me the two horses to hold. A minute later he was back, a cardboard box under each arm. Both boxes were full of books.

"What are those for?" I asked.

Jesse gave me a pitying look. "The more literate among us usually read them. But I suppose *you* might use them to cook your bacon and eggs if we ran out of firewood. Come on, Steve, think about it. It's dark longer than it's daylight this time of year. There's no wild current bushes up there to plug your TV into, so it's either reading or knitting."

I looked at the top layer. Jesse's old favorites, books I'd first seen in his truck and that he'd been nose-deep in for the last two evenings. Real exciting titles like *The Redesigned Forest* and *This Was Our Valley.* I wondered what color I should make my sweater.

Jesse set the books in the truck and turned to me. "Okay. One of us drives the truck, the other rides and leads the horses. Which do you want to do?"

I knew which I *wanted* to do. I'd take riding over bouncing along rough trails in a truck any day of the week. *Except* today. I'd woke up with my arm so sore it took me half an hour to get it loosened up enough that it didn't show I was favoring it. A few miles of riding and leading a couple of horses was just what I didn't need. "I'll take the truck."

"Thought you would," Jesse said with a grin I would have deeply enjoyed knocking off of his face.

There were a few last minute instructions from Carl and Connie about things like being careful and remembering to cook proper meals and then I was in the truck and Jesse was leading the way with the three horses moving out at a ground-eating trot. A couple of miles later we stopped for a gate and Jesse came over to my open window. "Okay," he said, "it's all straight ahead from here. All you have to do is follow the trail till you come to the cabin. You might as well go ahead. You can make better time. Start unloading when you get there. The key to the cabin is under the window ledge." I nodded and started to pull around him and the horses but he stopped me. "Hey, Steve!" I hit the brake and threw the truck into reverse.

"Yeah?" I said, sticking my head out as I came up beside him again.

"Check the gas gage, huh?" I floored it and Jesse's laughing face disappeared in a satisfying cloud of dust.

Fifteen minutes of rough trail later I came over the top of a hill and saw my vacation condo laid out below me. there was a wide grassy valley with a creek wandering through it. Among the pine and spruce groves scattered along the creek, bunches of fat cows lazily chewed their cuds. Others grazed on the dry fall grass or stood drinking from the creek. The cabin was at the near end of the valley, shaded by the biggest of the trees. It could have been a hundred years old the way its logs had weathered to a silvery gray and it seemed to have kind of sunk down to become a part of the land. The only other signs of civilization were an equally weathered log barn, a couple of corrals, and a fenced-off corner full of big, round bales of hay.

This had to be about the loneliest place in Alberta — and it was just what I'd been looking for. I opened the truck window, took in a big breath of that wild, free air and, for the first time in longer than I wanted to remember, felt myself start to relax. This was going to be okay. Nobody who could possibly be trouble even knew I was here except for Jesse Firelight. The thought of him got me moving again. If he got here before I even had the door open I'd never hear the last of it. I drove on down the hill.

The key was where he said it would be and the door creaked open with the sound of a mummy's tomb opening in a movie. A wave of cold, musty air came out to meet me. Something small skittered out of sight under a bunk. I hoped it was just a mouse. Stephen King would have had a great time with this place with its spiderwebs and cracked, smoky window panes. I shivered. What this place needed most was a good fire to warm it up. Okay, I could handle that. Any fool could build a fire in a woodstove.

I surveyed the big, black cookstove that crouched sulkily in one end of the single room. There was a pile of good, dry wood, kindling, and paper beside it. I lifted one of the lids off the stove, wadded up the sports section of a six-month-old Calgary Herald — after checking to see how the Flames were doing at that point — laid some kindling on top, opened the front draft, and touched a match to the paper. It burst into a crackling orange flame that lit up the whole room — and all the little brown things the mice had left scattered across the worn board floor. I closed the lid and went hunting for a broom. There didn't seem to be one in the cabin. Then I remembered seeing one somewhere among all the stuff in the back of the truck.

Naturally, the broom was under everything else. It took me a few minutes to dig it out. By the time I got back to the cabin the whole place was on fire. At least, if the saying, "Where there's smoke there's fire," is true the whole cabin *must* have been on fire. The billows of smoke were so thick I couldn't see a foot in front of me. Great! Jesse lets me out of his sight for fifteen minutes and I burn the cabin down.

Swishing the broom in front of me I managed to clear a path through the smoke to the stove. But another huge cloud billowed out, blinding me and sending me into a coughing fit. The cabin door had swung shut behind me. I groped my way over to the door, flung it wide open again, and, holding the broom upside down, started sweeping smoke-filled air out the door. My eyes were watering so bad I couldn't see. I just stood there in the doorway coughing my guts out and waving my broom.

Gradually, the air started to clear. I could breathe again. I rubbed my sleeve across my burning eyes and tried opening them. The first thing I saw was that the smoke inside the cabin was down to a blue haze. Then, I glanced outside. Not twenty feet away, Jesse sat on his roan, relaxed as a sack of potatoes, studying me with an expression like he was watching the Three Stooges. He caught my eye and grinned. "White man make smoke signal?"

I threw the broom at him. It missed. "There's a squirrel's nest or somethin' in the chimney," I managed to get out between coughs. "Get off that horse and come and help me before I drag you off and break your neck." It's hard to sound dangerous when you've got tears running down your face and your voice won't come out any louder than a strangled squeak, but when I started heading in his direction Jesse slid lazily off the horse.

"Okay, okay, city boy. Relax." He walked right over to the stove, reached up, and casually flicked a chrome-plated lever set into the stovepipe. "That should do it."

I stared at him. "What?"

He shook his head. "The things they don't teach you in delinquent school. It's called a damper, Steve. It closes off the chimney so once you've got a fire burning good you can keep it burning real slow for a long time. But you don't ever try to *start* a fire with it closed." He grinned wickedly. "It makes it smoke."

"No kiddin'," I said through my teeth, and broke out into another coughing fit.

Jesse just laughed. "No need to pout about it." He tapped the pack of cigarettes in my shirt pocket. "At least you didn't pay good money for this lungful of smoke." Before I could say anything he was heading for the door.

"Come on, let's get the horses put away. Then you can unpack the truck and *I'll* take care of the fire."

By noon the cabin was warm, as clean as it was going to get, and smelled only slightly like a smokehouse. We had something to eat and then went out to check some fence. It didn't take long to find a place by the creek where the beavers had cut a bunch of trees and let them fall right on top of the fence. All those big trees had to be cut up with the chain saw and moved out of the way. Then the broken wire had to be spliced and stretched and new posts pounded in.

It was mid-afternoon when I sawed the last length off the last tree. I switched off the saw, wiped the sweat off my face, and stood listening to the silence. But not for long. Jesse was in the middle of driving a big, sturdy post into the ground with the heavy post mall. The crack echoed across the hillside each time the heavy head of the mall connected with the top of the post. He hit that post four or five more times, stepped back and studied it, and must have decided it was good enough. Then he noticed me standing there watching him. "Hey, city boy," he called, breathing hard, "the score's four to nothing."

"What?"

"I just selfishly pounded four of these posts without ever stopping to think you might like a turn. Fortunately, there's one left. And it's all yours." His face was in the shadows but I caught the flash of his teeth as he grinned.

"Can't wait," I said. I walked over and he handed me the post mall. I slid the polished wooden handle back and forth through my hands gingerly, testing the weight.

Jesse gave me an amused look and then picked up the last fence post. He lined it up with the others, and stuck the sharpened point in the ground. Then he stepped back. "It's all yours," he said.

I took a deep breath, tightened my grip on the handle, and raised the post mall above my head. Then I gritted my teeth, slammed the heavy head down on top of the post as hard as I could — and just about passed out.

Jesse shook his head. "For somebody who knows about fencing you sure do have an awkward way of going about it. I suppose when it came to pounding posts all you ever had to do was pull the levers on a hydraulic pounder, huh, city boy?"

"You got that right," I lied. I'd been pounding posts by hand all fall. I just hadn't been doing it with a bullet hole in my arm.

"Try it again."

I rearranged my grip, trying to take most of the weight with my left arm. Jesse caught me. "No, not like that. Put your right hand here where it'll do some good. Like this." He rearranged my grip again.

I shook him off. "Leave me alone, Jesse. I'm left-handed. Left-handed people do things opposite to right-handed ones. All you're doin' is messin' me up." I took another swing. The impact shook me a lot more than it did the post. But I managed two more swings before Jesse ran out of patience. He reached for the post mall.

"Ground'll freeze up in a month or so," he said. "Hate to see you still working on that post when that happens." He drove it into the ground with two powerful swings.

I just stood there and tried not to look grateful.

Seven

By the time we finished supper it was getting dark. Jesse lit the kerosene lamp on the table and then dragged out his books and settled down to read in the feeble circle of light. I paced around, studying points of interest in the one-roomed cabin. That took about two minutes. I put some wood in the stove, stared out the window for a while at the big orange harvest moon just climbing above the eastern horizon, made a trip outside and down the path to the toilet, which had been taken over by a squirrel and was about half-full of spruce cones, came back in, had a drink of water, put some wood in the stove, stared out the window some more, rearranged the groceries on the shelves, paced around some more . . .

"Sit!" Jesse's voice was calm but commanding, just right for obedience classes.

"Woof!" I said, and sat down. "Want me to beg, too?"

Jesse pushed back strand of hair, took a deep breath, and said, very slowly and clearly, "What I want is for you to quit pacing around here like a caged tiger before you drive me completely out of my mind."

"Wouldn't take much gas for that trip," I muttered.

"Look," he said, "I told you evenings were going to be like this. And they're only going to get longer and darker. You have to find yourself something to do." His eyes swept the room and came to rest on a battered, old black-covered book lying on a shelf by the table. He picked it up and tossed it to me. "Here, you might learn something. Don't move until you've read it all the way through."

I looked at the book. *Common Ailments of the Cow* it said in faded gold letters on the cover. I looked at Jesse to see if he was kidding. He wasn't. I opened the book and looked at the first page.

"Jesse," I said, "this book was published in 1929."

Jesse smiled and nodded. "And I think you'll find that, unlike the automobile, the latest model of the trusty cow still has the same basic chassis, motor, and exhaust system she did in 1929. Go on, read it. It's even got pictures."

I sighed, pulled up a chair on the opposite side of the table and got on with my homework.

Two hours later I closed the book. I now knew more about the inside of a cow than I had ever wanted to know. Jesse was still totally absorbed in his reading, and it was only nine-thirty. I decided I needed something to eat so I made myself a sandwich. "Want one?" I asked Jesse.

He didn't even look up. "Later," he muttered.

I poured myself some coffee and sat down in a chair by the stove. I was half done the sandwich when there was a movement in the shadows under the bottom bunk. I sat like a statue and stared hard at the spot. Sure enough, something moved. Then I caught the gleam of the eyes and gradually a little grayish-brown body took shape. My friend the mouse had returned. He was sitting just under the edge of the bunk now, staring at me just as hard as I was staring at him. Real slow, I broke off a chunk of my sandwich and tossed it over toward the mouse. He panicked and skittered out of sight. I waited. Sure enough, a couple of minutes later he was back. He crept up on the bread like he was about to defuse a live bomb then suddenly grabbed it and shot out of sight with it. I threw another chunk, not quite so far this time . . .

I was down to my last crumb and the mouse was collecting it from so close I could have touched him with my foot when I felt eyeballs burning into the side of my head. I looked up. I was pretty sure that from where Jesse was sitting all he could see was me gradually dismantling my food and tossing it, one piece at a time, across the floor. "Just feeding the mouse," I said.

Jesse shook his head and sighed. "Of all the people in the world, I wind up with a roommate who socializes with rodents."

I grinned. "He's better company than you are."

I didn't expect to sleep much that night — the bunk was lumpy and my arm was aching. But I was so tired I went to sleep fast and stayed asleep. Well, except for waking up once to the pitter-patter of cold little feet stomping across my face. Socializing with rodents at two a.m. was pushing things a little far. I was beginning to understand why Jesse had claimed the top bunk.

Next morning we spread out a couple of bales of hay to get the cows used to coming for feed. Then we rode around the boundaries of the lease. It was bigger than I'd realized. Over three thousand acres that took in just about every kind of country there was — open meadows where the grass grew tall and thick, swamps full of slough grass, pine-covered ridges that didn't grow much grass at all but smelled like a Christmas tree convention. And everywhere there were animals. Moose lifting their big, ugly noses out of the sloughs to stare unconcerned as we rode by, deer bouncing off into the brush at the sound of our horses, elk grazing on a hillside and not even looking up as we rode by. Once, a coyote loped through the tall slough grass, looking like just a pair of ears skimming along above the grass. The more I saw of this country the better I liked it. So much I even admitted it to Jesse when we finally pulled up at the farthest corner of the lease. "I didn't know there were still places this wild left," I said.

Jesse gave me a look I couldn't read. Like he was taking in what I'd said but something else was on his mind. Then, he slid off his horse and opened the gate out of the grazing lease.

"You think *this* is wild country?" His voice was edged with a cold anger I'd never heard from Jesse before. "You haven't seen wild country yet. I'll show you country you'll never forget." I kept quiet and followed him through the gate. Whatever this trip was about, it beat fencing.

We must have ridden for two or three hours, due west. Jesse was right. The country *did* get wilder. Wilder and higher. The ridges were rockier now, the valleys deeper. The mountains that had always been there like distant castles in the west leaned closer now, shadowing the land. It was only mid-afternoon but already the sun was sliding behind them. I was beginning to wonder how much farther we could ride without ending up spending the night out here under the stars. Then, the trail took a steep upward pitch that had the horses puffing as they dug in and scrambled up the slope.

The trail turned, steepened again, and all of a sudden we were on top. On top of the ridge — and on top of the world. Below us spread the most untouched valley I'd ever seen. Winding between the big, rock-topped foothills as far as you could see a river made a silver ribbon in the solid green of ancient forest, then finally disappeared into a hazy gap in the mountains. Hundreds of acres of trees. No highways, no cutlines, no ski resorts. Just wilderness, the way this whole country must have looked a couple of hundred years ago.

"The Wolfsong Valley," Jesse said softly. We sat on our horses in silence for a long time, just taking in the scene below. Lady reached down and gave her sweaty nose a good itching on her front leg, then gave herself a noisy all-over shake. That broke the silence. I turned to Jesse. "You're right," I said. "I won't forget this."

"Yeah? Well you better memorize it now, city boy. 'Cause it won't be here much longer," Jesse turned to look at me, his face so hard it looked like a bronze statue.

"What?"

"You see the white water there where the river's running fast and rough over the rocks?"

"Yeah?"

"That's where the gas plant's going to be."

"A gas plant? Out here in the middle of nowwhere? Where they gonna get the gas?"

"Pipeline runs along on the other side of that next range of hills. Dead easy to run it on over here."

"Aw come on, Jesse, they're not gonna build a plant out here in the middle of all these trees."

"Trees? What trees? They're going to clear-cut the whole valley first. Double economic benefit for the oil industry and the lumber industry. Should be good for lots of votes."

I stared out over the valley. "No, Jesse, it's not gonna happen. They can't destroy a place like this just to make a few bucks. Too many people will fight it."

Jesse laughed at me. "You ever see what they did to the Old Man River? People fought that, too."

I didn't know what to say. And I didn't know the hard-faced, bitter man sitting here beside me. He turned to look at me again. "Oh, yeah, there's one other thing. It's sour gas they're going to process here, hydrogen sulphide in it, the deadliest, most polluting stuff the devil ever invented. If it ever blows . . ." His voice trailed off. Then he added, "That's one reason the big guys think this is the ideal place for the plant. Nothing out here worth worrying about."

"Jesse, somehow I get the feeling this valley means something more personal to you than just one more piece of wilderness the politicians want to pave."

Jesse's gaze swept out over the valley again, his eyes following a hawk that soared high above the silver river below. "Yeah." His voice was soft. "I guess it is personal."

There was a long silence. "You gonna tell me about it, Jess?"

"Why should I?"

"'Cause then I might understand about your valley."

Jesse took a long, slow breath. "I got messed up pretty bad when I was a kid. Bad enough that I just about quit caring what happened to me. I didn't know who I really was anymore, where I belonged, what I wanted to be." His voice trailed off and for a minute he just sat there looking out over the valley while his fingers untangled knots in Firebird's mane. Then he went on. "Finally I couldn't stand it any longer. I'd read about how, in the old days, young warriors used to go out in the wilderness alone and stay there till they got some kind of vision of their life. So, I took off with just a canteen of water, a bag of beef jerky, and a couple of blankets, and headed west. I didn't know — or care — where I was going. Maybe I was secretly hoping I'd die out there somewhere. I walked all day and, just at sunset, I made it to the top of this ridge. And as I sat here and watched the sun disappear behind the mountains a huge bull elk came across the ridge and stood silhouetted against the red sky and an owl hooted in the distance and right then I knew this place would always be special to me."

Jesse laughed softly. "Sorry, city boy, I didn't mean to bore you with a speech," he said, sounding embarrassed.

"I'm not bored," I said honestly. "There were places out on the coast I felt that way about." Shut up, Steve, a voice inside me warned. Just keep on listening but don't start talking about yourself. "So, was that the vision you were looking for?"

Jesse thought for a minute. "Yes and no. It was never real mystic like I read about, spirit voices and all that supernatural stuff. But, I spent five days out here and by the time I went home I knew who I was and what mattered to me. I guess that's as close to a vision as most people ever come."

I just nodded. I sure wished I could come that close.

We sat silently for a minute looking out across the valley. Then, Jesse swung his horse around. "Let's get out of here. I've got no business bringing you up here on the boss's time. Got no business bringing you up here at all." Suddenly he touched his spurs to Firebird's sides and the big horse plunged down the steep hill in a spray of gravel.

"Jesse, hold on — " But he was already out of sight around the bend and Lady was about to have a fit at being left behind. I gave up and loosened the reins.

It was a mile or so later before I finally caught Jesse. He was halfway up a long hill, leading his sweating, winded horse. I slid off Lady, loosened her cinch so she could get her wind better, and fell into step beside him. Jesse just kept looking straight ahead and something in his face told me not to try and start a conversation. At the top of the hill we climbed back on the horses. It was a long, slow, dead-quiet ride home.

After supper Jesse buried himself in the books again. This time I took a closer look at the titles. And one small link in the puzzle that was Jesse Firelight snapped together. The way he read all those books on pollution and forests and conserving the environment, it was no wonder Jesse had got so choked about the gas plant. Or had he started reading the books *after* he found out about the plant? And what good did he think reading about it was going to do anyhow?

But I knew better than to ask him. I resigned myself to another evening of *Common Ailments of the Cow*.

Eight

By morning Jesse was his usual cheerful, irritating self again as he dragged me out of bed before daylight for a fun morning of fencing. We loaded up all the tools and rode the fence lines again looking for trouble. It wasn't hard to find. Between trees falling on top of the fences and moose and elk charging right through them, there were plenty of holes to fix.

Just before noon Jesse pounded in a staple, breathed a big sigh, and started packing up. "That's it, city boy. Quittin' time."

I stared at him. "Since when is eleven-thirty quittin' time?"

"Since today's Thursday. I get Thursday afternoons off."

"Yeah? Do I get them off, too?"

"Nope. Somebody's got to stay here and mind the store. You pick a different day off."

We rode the rest of the way home in silence. After we'd looked after the horses and eaten a sorry-looking sandwich, Jesse washed and rebraided his hair and put on his best jeans, a clean shirt, and buckskin jacket I'd never seen him wear before.

"Where you goin'?" I asked. He picked up a little leather suitcase and headed for the door.

"Indian business, city boy." He gave me one of those unreadable looks of his over his shoulder and walked out.

I followed him out the door. "So what am I supposed to do?"

He shrugged. "Well, you could take advantage of the fact that nobody's here to watch you and just do nothing, or," a hint of a grin twitched the corners of his mouth, "you could impress me half to death by taking a shovel up to that spring I showed you on the southwest quarter and digging out all the mud and sludge to make a half-decent waterhole out of it."

Jesse climbed in the truck. Then he opened the window and just sat there staring at me for a minute. "You okay?" he said.

I stared back at him. "Why wouldn't I be okay?"

He shrugged. "You just look kind of funny."

Come to think of it, I wasn't feeling all that great. After a morning of stretching wire and pounding in staples — Jesse had gone ahead and pounded all the posts himself — my arm was aching again and I felt lousy all over. But I wasn't about to let on.

Jesse started the engine. "See you tonight, city boy. Try and stay out of trouble while you're sitting in the sunshine, huh?" The truck bounced away over the rough trail and disappeared behind the hill.

I stared at the lingering cloud of dust for a long time. Choice number one was real tempting. I sat down in the sun by the side of the cabin and watched the clouds sail by for a while. But I kept getting a mental picture of Jesse coming home and finding out I'd done just exactly what he knew I would. And that told-you-so look he was going to have on his face made me so mad I dragged myself to my feet, saddled up, and headed west with a shovel in my hand.

I'd never dug out a spring before — and I don't ever plan on digging one out again. It's like standing in a huge bowl of ice-cold porridge shoveling out more ice-cold porridge and throwing it over your shoulder while more porridge seeps right back into the hole you thought you dug. And all the time, your feet are sinking deeper and deeper into the porridge and you're remembering every movie you ever saw that featured death by quicksand.

I spent the whole afternoon like that, in my bare feet — my boots were the only decent piece of clothing I owned and I wasn't about to sacrifice them — with my jeans rolled up past my knees like a loco grape stomper, freezing from the knees down in the icy mud and sweating from the knees up in the hot sun. But I finally got the spring opened up and hauled a bunch of big rocks down the hill to keep the cows from stomping the mud back into the waterhole again. Then I washed my ice-blue feet in the cold spring, put my boots back on, grabbed my shovel, and gratefully — and carelessly — climbed on Lady.

I guess that was the moment she'd been waiting for all week. The next thing I knew her nose was between her front toes, her hind feet were raking the sky, and I was loosely connected with her bow-shaped back somewhere in between. I'd stayed on a few horses that could buck better than that black mare — but never with a shovel in my hand. I dropped the shovel. But by then it was too late to get my balance back. I landed in a big patch of rose bushes. I thought the horse would light out for home and leave me walking but she didn't. She just looked back over her shoulder with the satisfied expression of somebody who had just made a point. And I had got the point. Several of them, in fact. I climbed back on, carefully, but Lady never even twitched, and spent the ride home picking thorns out of various parts of me.

The sun was down before I got back to the cabin and the wind had turned around to the north and had a bite in it. By the time I got Lady put away and a fire on in the cabin I was shivering. I supposed I should get something to eat but I didn't feel like eating. To tell you the truth, I was starting to feel downright lousy, hot and cold and kind of light-headed like maybe I was coming down with the flu. At least, that was what I hoped it was. But I wasn't so sure. For a couple of days my arm had seemed to be getting better but now it was hurting a lot again. I hoped it was just because I'd been using it too much. I pulled off my shirt, undid the bandage, and had a look at the wound. My upper arm was kind of red and hot but the bullet holes had scabbed over and seemed to be healing okay. I rinsed the bandage in cold water and wrapped it around my arm again. Then I pulled my boots off and crawled into my bunk.

I don't know how long I slept. It was either the wind or the pain in my arm that woke me. Both of them were howling pretty good by then. I was sweating and dizzy as I stumbled out of bed in the darkness and stood staring at the luminous face of the alarm clock on the table. It was nearly two o'clock in the morning. Where was Jesse? He said he was going to be back tonight. Then I looked out the window — and decided I must be delirious. Snow had drifted halfway up the window and solid white sheets of it whirled past on the screaming wind. But then I remembered the dark ridge of clouds in the north this afternoon and the knife-edged wind that had been blowing. Even if this was just October the snow was real enough. Too real. Because right then it hit me why Jesse wasn't back yet. He wasn't coming back. Not tonight.

Even the four-by-four would never make it through those rock-hard, bumper-deep drifts. Nobody would be getting in or out of here for at least a couple of days. I was on my own.

And that's when I started to get scared. Because every heartbeat felt like somebody was working his way through my arm with a jackhammer and I knew it was time to quit kidding myself. I had a rip-roaring infection in that bullet wound and it wasn't about to go away.

My hand was shaking so bad it took three matches to get the lamp lighted. The tight-stretched skin of my swollen upper arm shone dully in the pale, golden light. It was burning hot to touch. But the worst part was the red lines edging their way up toward my shoulder. Blood poisoning. Blood poisoning killed you if you didn't do something about it — fast.

I staggered over to the water pail and got a drink. The water was cold. Then I realized the whole cabin was cold. The fire had been out for hours. And I was still burning up. Oh, God, I was sick. I'd been beat up, knifed, tramped on by horses, and in a car accident or two but I'd never felt this bad. Not even in the detox center when they made me quit the dope cold turkey. All right, so this was it. End of the line. I didn't really care. I just wanted it to be over fast.

I was sitting on the bunk staring across the cabin at nothing and then, all of a sudden, I realized I was staring at *something*. Jesse's rifle, hanging there above the door where it always was. Without thinking what I was doing I stumbled over and carefully lifted it down with my left hand. I sat down at the table with it. The gun smelled like oil and powder. The barrel gleamed softly in the lamplight. I picked up the rifle and laid my burning face against the polished wood of the stock. It felt cool, comforting, like a friend.

No. That was too easy. I hadn't fought this long and this hard to stay alive to give up now. I laid the gun down and staggered to my feet. Maybe I was going out this time but I was going out fighting. I threw a blanket around my shoulders, grabbed a flashlight, and stumbled out into the storm.

I shone the light on the line of fence posts that led off over the hill and toward the ranch. There wasn't a hope in hell I'd made it down there but at least I was going to die trying. The wind-whipped snow felt good against my hot face. I stumbled in a drift and went down. Cool snow wrapped its arms around me, numbing the pain a little. They say freezing to death isn't such a bad way to go.

I got up and kept going. I edged around the corner of the barn and a full blast of wind almost knocked me over. Then, something *did* knock me over. I knocked it over, too. It was shaped like a human being but completely covered with snow. An abominable snowman, said a fevered voice in my head. "Jesse?" I gasped out loud. He shook himself like a wet dog, sending snow flying all over the place. "Who were you expecting?" he muttered sourly, "Santa Claus?"

For a minute we both just lay there, staring at each other's outline in the drifting snow. Then Jesse struggled to his feet. "Well, come on, let's get inside. I didn't make it this far to freeze to death beside the barn."

He reached a hand out to me. I took it and managed to drag myself out of the snow "Where's the truck?" I yelled, my voice nearly lost in the screaming wind.

"Buried to the bumpers in that steep draw a couple miles back."

Holding on to each other we staggered through the drifts back to the cabin. We were just outside the door when I collapsed into Jesse's arms. He held me up with one hand, pushed the door open with the other, and half-dragged me inside. "Steve? You okay?" he asked, his voice puzzled.

I pulled in a deep breath. "No," I whispered. I sank into a chair beside the table, laid my head on the table, and closed my eyes. There was a long moment of silence. "Steve?"

"What?"

"How come the rifle's on the table?"

I didn't answer.

"Steve?"

"Thought I saw a bear out there," I muttered, still not raising my head.

Long pause. "What color bear?"

I groaned. I didn't care what color. I didn't even know why I lied to Jesse in the first place. "White," I grated out between clenched teeth.

Another long, long pause. I could feel Jesse's eyes on me but I wouldn't look up. Finally I heard him pick up the rifle and hang it up. "Yeah," he said slowly, "that'd be one of those Pincher Creek Polar Bears. We get'em up here whenever it snows at Hallowe'en." He pulled the blanket off my shoulders and I heard him give a low whistle. "Sit up," he said gently, "let's have a look at that arm."

Nine

*J*esse reached out and touched the swollen flesh around the scabbed-over bullet holes. "Don't, Jess!" I gasped, jerking away so hard I almost fell off the chair. I sat there waiting for the waves of pain to subside — and, now that Jesse had seen the wound, waiting for him to ask the inevitable question.

But, he didn't. He just shook his head. "You are one sick puppy, Steve," he said, his voice gentle. "How long has it been like this?"

I tried to shrug but it came out lopsided because I could only move one shoulder. "Just started gettin' bad today."

Jesse shook his head. "You've got a impressive infection there, you know."

"Glad you like it," I muttered.

"I don't know if I can do anything with this. You need a doctor."

I looked up at him. "Yeah." My voice came out in a hoarse whisper. "But right now you're all I've got, Jess."

We looked at each other for what seemed like a long

time. Finally Jesse nodded, "Okay, city boy, I'll do what I can." He turned away and began layering paper and kindling in the old woodstove.

I laid my head back down on the table, cushioned on my good arm, and watched him. A question had been running around in the back of my foggy brain ever since I bumped into Jesse out in the storm. Now the mist had cleared enough to remember what it was. "Jess?"

"Yeah," he muttered, concentrating on touching a match to the paper.

"Why'd you come back here tonight? You could've just stayed at the ranch when it started stormin' so bad instead of risking your life fightin' your way up here."

Jesse put the lid on the stove. "What? And miss out on your charming company?" he said with a teasing grin.

My eyes stayed locked on his. "Why *really*, Jess?"

Jesse's face turned serious — and maybe a little embarrassed. "Because I couldn't stop thinking about the way you looked when I left. Like there was something really wrong." He turned to fill a kettle with water. Then his eyes met mine again. "'Cause I was worried about you, city boy, is that okay?" His voice was real gentle.

"Yeah, Jess," I said with a deep sigh as some of the fear drained out of me, "it's okay." I still figured I was probably going to die but if I had to have just one person between me and dying in a blizzard in the middle of nowhere I'd just as soon take my chances on Jesse Firelight.

I watched him stoke the fire and get the water boiling. He seemed a long ways away, like maybe I was watching him on TV or something. I drifted in and out of consciousness, scared to let the darkness take over in case I never woke up again, scared to come back to full consciousness where the pain would be waiting.

Jesse took something shiny out of his pocket. A jack-knife. He was good with that knife. I'd seen him use it for everything from picking a stone out of Firebird's hoof to castrating a late-born bull calf. I couldn't decide if those memories reassured me or scared me half to death.

I watched as he got out a whetstone and sharpened the knife. My eyes followed each lazy circle of steel against stone, making me even dizzier than I already was. Maybe I'd seen too many Civil War movies. "Jess," I said weakly, "you ain't plannin' an amputation are you?"

Jesse laughed grimly. "Not exactly." But if I don't get that wound opened up and let the poison out, that could be Plan B."

In spite of the fact I was boiling hot and sweating like a pig I felt a cold shiver run through me.

Jesse set the knife down and went to dig around in the top of the cupboard where the ear tags and stuff were kept. He came back with a dusty old dark brown bottle about a quarter full of liquid. I eyed it warily. Then with a surge of relief I realized what it must be. Whiskey. This was going to be like in the old western movies. Before the doctor starts cutting, the patient downs a big slug of whiskey and never feels a thing. I waited for Jesse to hand over the bottle. But instead he got some hot water off the stove, poured it into the wash basin, and then dumped a shot from the bottle in, too. Hey, that wasn't the way it was supposed to go. I was just getting up the strength to say that when the smell of the steam from the basin hit me. And it didn't smell like whiskey. If my problem had been clogged sinuses I'd have been cured already. I stared hard at the bottle's faded label. Cicalin Disinfectant. Good old traditional antiseptic for everything from wire cuts to hoof rot. Great stuff — if you're a cow. Personally, I'd rather have the whiskey.

Jesse rinsed the knife blade in the basin. Then he gave me one of his unreadable looks. "Too bad you're not an Indian." he said.

I gave him kind of a glazed glare. "What's that got to do with anythin'?"

"An Indian would hold still for this."

That made me mad. I raised my head and looked him in the eye. "I'll hold sti . . ." I began, but, before my dazed reflexes could figure out what was happening Jesse's hand made a lightning-fast arc and the knife's razor-edge slashed deep into the swollen flesh between the two scabbed-over wounds.

I screamed. But I held still — mainly because it was all over before I could move. Then, the relief was almost as powerful as the pain as a hot stream of blood and pus exploded over my arm and some of the unbelievable pressure inside started to ease away. Jesse let it bleed some.

Then he soaked a rag in the Creolin solution, held the cut open wide, and dripped a bunch of that stuff inside. I hated him a lot by the time he finished that and I figured he'd be wearing my fingernail prints in his wrist for a while.

I laid my head on the table and shut my eyes again as he bandaged the whole mess up in an old dish towel. Vaguely, I heard him opening the trap door to the dirt cellar below the cabin. Now what? As far as I knew the only thing down there was a sack of potatoes we kept where it was cool.

When I opened my eyes again Jesse was back. He had a little brown bottle in one hand and a syringe in the other. The next thing I knew he'd scrubbed a patch on my good arm and jabbed in a needle that felt a whole lot duller than his knife had been. I jumped. "What was that?" I muttered.

"Penicillin."

"You always keep penicillin on hand in case somebody gets blood poisoning in a blizzard?"

"Nope."

"What d'you mean, 'nope'? Where'd it come from then?"

"It was here. It's just not *people* penicillin."

I sat up a little straighter. "What?"

The corners of Jesse's mouth twitched a little. "It's cow penicillin. We keep it on hand to treat sick critters."

I sat up *real* straight. "Thanks a lot, Firelight! As if I ain't sick enough you go givin' me cow medicine! You trying to kill me or what?" I started to stand up but Jesse caught me just as the room started to sway back and forth kind of violently.

"Settle down, city boy, penicillin's penicillin. It won't do you any harm. Might even do some good if you're lucky." He grinned. "Anyhow, at the very least we won't have to worry about you coming down with hoof rot." Before I could say anything he was dragging me the rest of the way to my feet. "Come on, you better lie down before you fall down," he said, leading me over to my bunk.

"I ain't gonna fall down, Firelight," I muttered, hanging onto him good and tight so I didn't make myself a liar. He lowered me gently onto the bunk and threw a blanket over me. I threw it off again. I had enough of a fever to keep me warm naked in a snowbank.

Jesse shook his head. "I can see you're going to be a real fun patient." He sounded real tired.

"Yeah?" I said, wishing I had the strength to get my voice above a whisper. His face kept floating in and out of a red mist. "Well, trust me, Firelight, you're a real fun doctor, too." Maybe it would be easier to quit fighting and drift with the mist. I closed my eyes.

"Steve? You still awake?"

"Mmm," I said from some faraway country on the edge of unconsciousness.

"You want to tell me how you happened to get shot?"

My eyes flickered open. For a second they met Jesse's.

"Not really," I whispered. I closed my eyes and crossed the border.

Ten

I woke up slow, too tired to even open my eyes at first and feeling real lousy. If I was going to have a hangover this bad at least I should remember the party. But I couldn't even remember where I was. I forced my eyes open and found myself staring at the bare wooden beams above. *Still* didn't know where I was.

Then, I tried to sit up. My whole right side felt like it had been under a rockslide for a few days. I focused on my upper arm, red and swollen and wrapped in a strip of grayish-white dish towel. Dr. Firelight's work. Now I remembered. I looked around the cabin for Jesse but he wasn't there. He couldn't have been gone long. A fire crackled in the belly of the old stove and a pot of coffee sat steaming on top of it. Suddenly my brain locked onto the smell of that coffee the way a heat-seeking missile locks onto the exhaust of a jet. I'd just found a good enough reason to drag myself out of bed.

I threw off the blanket and, relieved to see my jeans were still on, stood up — and almost fell flat on my face. I grabbed the edge of the bunk for support and, when the earth stabilized a little, staggered weakly over to the stove. As I poured the coffee my hand was shaking so bad I thought I was going to scald myself and needed more of Dr. Firelight's veterinary care. I shuddered and poured real careful.

Definitely Jesse's coffee, I thought, wincing at the first swallow. But I sank into a chair and drank two cups before I stopped shaking and started wondering what it was about the scene outside the window that was driving me crazy. Everything looked fine out there. Lots of bright fall sunshine. Greenish grass just about faded out to brown. A few puddles shining in the sun. Just a normal late fall day.

Suddenly, it clicked. *That's* what was wrong with it. It wasn't supposed to be normal. When I stumbled out the door and into Jesse it had been a raging blizzard out there. Where was the snow? And how *long* had I been unconscious?

I had to find Jesse.

I stepped outside and just stood there leaning against the door frame, partly because I was too weak to go any farther for a while and partly because just standing in the sunshine and breathing fresh air felt so good. God, it was great to be alive.

I had to find Jesse.

It wasn't hard. The sound of hammering led me around the side of the cabin and then I saw him down by the barn, putting a new shoe on Firebird. He was bent over with his back to me and couldn't see me coming so I just leaned against a tree and watched. He hammered in the last couple of nails, cut off the ends, and clinched them, now and then softly cussing or complimenting the horse. Then, without raising his voice, he said, "So, I see you decided to live after all."

It took me a minute to realize he was talking to me.

"All you Indians got eyes in the back of your heads or what? How'd you know I was here?"

Jesse kept on with his work. "Firebird told me."

I let that sink in. Okay, I did see the horse swivel an ear back to check me out as I walked up. Old Jesse didn't miss much. He let Firebird put his foot down and went around front to file off the rough spots where the nails came out the top of the hoof.

"Jess, what day is it?"

"Saturday," he said absently, still filing.

I tried to think my way through that. What day was the blizzard? Thursday? Yeah. Thursday was Jesse's day off. But things still didn't add up. "What date is it?"

"The second. Stop that, Firebird."

My brain processed that. "Of November?"

Jesse gave a deep sigh, laid down his file and looked up at me. "Yeah, Spaceman, November. We're still in the twentieth century and the planet's Earth. You only slept about a day and a half. What'd you think? You landed in the middle of *Back to the Future* or something?"

Still confused, I gazed around the muddy corral. I guess I was even sicker than I realized that night, hallucinating big-time. But it had seemed so real.

"Jesse," I said cautiously, "What happened to the snow?"

Jesse straightened up, rubbed his back, and pulled the halter off the horse. "Okay, get out of here you ugly knothead, and if you lose that shoe you're coming back in a can of Dr. Ballard's, you hear?" He spoke gruffly — but I noticed him slipping the roan a lump of sugar at the same time. Then he turned to me. "Haven't been in Alberta long, have you, city boy?"

"I was born here. But I've been away a while."

"Long enough to forget about Alberta chinooks? It quit snowing about four yesterday morning. At seven the wind was howling so loud I looked out to see if it was storming again and saw water dripping off the roof. By the time I could quit babysitting you long enough to go back for the truck the drift it was in was mostly melted — now the truck's stuck to the hubcaps in mud."

That did make sense when I stopped to think about it. Chinooks did some wild and crazy things. Pop used to tell a joke about an old homesteader driving to town one day when a chinook hit. The horses were running in snow, the sleigh they were pulling was dragging in the mud, and the dog running behind was raising dust.

Then something else Jesse had said hit me. "What do you mean, babysittin' me? I've been out like a light ever since you put me to bed. I didn't need much babysittin'."

Jesse laughed. "That's what you think."

I stared at him. "Meanin' what?"

Jesse bent to pick up his tools. "Know anybody named Romero?" he asked casually.

My stomach tightened. "Why?" I said, too fast. "Did I say somethin' about Romero?"

"Didn't really *say* all that much. But three times during the first night when you were out of your head with the fever I had to drag you back to bed when you set out to go kill him."

I let out a long sigh. Keeping the past buried was hard enough work when I was wide awake. And totally impossible if I was gonna go and get delirious. I gave Jesse a weak grin. "Guess I didn't get him, huh?"

He laughed softly. "Nope, but for somebody with one foot in the grave and the other slipping you put up a pretty fair flight. But the third time you managed to fall on your face before I heard you. That time when I laid you down you stayed down. And I spent the rest of the night packing garbage bags of snow around you to cool you down and pumping penicillin into you." He stopped talking and gave me a hard look. "Time to get you back inside before you fall over on me again," he said, coming over to throw an arm around my waist. "You're too heavy to keep carrying back to bed. Anyway you're about due for another dose of penicillin."

I groaned. "Aw, Jess, not that blunt-nosed needle again. My left arm's already just about as sore as my right."

Jesse grinned. "Okay, we'll find a meatier part of your anatomy this time."

"Never mind, Jess, my arm'll do just fine."

I got more penicillin. *Where* I got it, I'm not about to discuss. Then Jesse made me lie down again while he warmed up some stew for me. But, just about the time he was ready to dish it up I fell asleep again.

When I woke up I knew instantly I was a lot better. I was still good and sore but not as weak or light-headed as before. And hungry enough to eat anything I could lay my hands on — even Jesse's stew. Jesse wasn't around so I started to get up and go help myself. Then, I heard voices outside. We had company. I laid back down, shut my eyes, and was doing a pretty good imitation of a possum as the door opened and two sets of footsteps came inside.

The footsteps stopped and for a minute nobody said anything but I could feel myself being stared at. Then, Carl's voice, almost a whisper, said, "He sure does look pale, all right. How long did you say he's been sick?"

Jesse's voice. "It's been a couple of days now. Guess he must have caught one of those Asian flu bugs that's been going around."

I heard Carl take a step closer. "I dunno. He doesn't look too good. You think we should haul him out and have a doctor take a look at him?"

Right then I came real close to yelling "Oh, no you don't!" but I managed to settle for grinding my teeth.

There was a long pause during which I tried to decide if I could make it out the door before one of them grabbed me. "No," Jesse said slowly, "the fever's broken. I think he'll survive. You know how these punk drifters are, half-starved and run-down from living on junk food and cigarettes. A little fresh air and clean living should fix him up." I ground my teeth a little more. Jesse was enjoying this too much.

Carl's heavy footsteps retreated. "All right, Jesse. I'll be up with a load of salt for the cows in a couple of days. Let me know if the kid gets any worse before then." The door opened and the footsteps moved outside. The door closed behind them. But the window was wide open and I could still hear every word from outside. Carl was talking again. "By the way, Jesse, I meant to ask. Is the kid worth having around when he *is* healthy?"

"I've seen worse. He's good with horses. A little green with cows but he'll learn. Altogether he's a little less trouble than a blizzard in calving season."

Carl chuckled. "Well, I hope he turns out to be worth all your babysitting. There was something about him I kinda took to. Seemed like he might be a good enough kid that's run into a lot of bad breaks."

"Yeah," Jesse said, "I'd say he's done that, all right."

"See you, Jesse." Saddle leather squeaked and there was the sound of hoofbeats as Carl headed his horse for home.

The door opened. Then Jesse's voice, cool and amused. "Okay, city boy, coast's clear. You can open your eyes now."

I did — and gave him a dirty look. "All right," I said, sitting up. "How'd you know this time?"

"That you weren't asleep?" Jesse asked with something close to a grin. "You'd better stay away from poker, city boy. Even with your eyes closed you telegraph what few thoughts happen to cross your mind. Every time some-body said something you didn't like a muscle in your jaw tightened up and made your dimples show. It was actually kind of cute."

I grabbed one of my boots off the floor and winged it at him. My aim was way off. The boot missed and landed in the water pail — and the movement sent a shot of pain through my arm that made me groan.

"You deserved that," Jessie said. "And this." He tossed my dripping boot back to land on the floor beside me. "If you're feeling so bright-eyed and bushy-tailed you can get up to the table. I saved your stew for you." I groaned again. But I ate it. Jesse ate, too, and then we sat watching the early November dusk fall.

"Jess?" He looked at me but I dropped my eyes to study my coffee cup for a while. This didn't come easy for me. At last I looked up and met his eyes. "Uh, thanks, Jess." I felt real awkward. "For what you did the other night — and for lyin' to Carl for me just now."

Jesse shrugged. "You'd have lied for yourself if you'd had the chance."

I studied his emotionless face, trying to figure out what was behind that statement — but Jesse could have made a lot of money at poker. "I didn't lie to you about much."

"Didn't tell me much truth, either."

I shifted uncomfortably under his level gaze. Those dark eyes of his had a way of looking right into your soul. And my soul was no tourist attraction.

"Okay. I owe you. What is it you want to know so bad?"

Jesse sipped his coffee. "All right," he said slowly, "let's try this one again. Who shot you?"

I took a deep breath. There was no hope of passing out this time. "Carlos Romero."

Jesse nodded. "I remember him. The guy you wanted to kill in the middle of the night. Why'd he shoot you?"

I lit my last cigarette and took a drag before I answered. But my voice still came out bitter. " 'Cause he wants me dead just as bad as I want him dead."

Jesse tried again. "So it's Romero, not the cops you're hiding out from?"

I shook my head. I was getting real tired again. "Both," I said. "I was in jail in B.C. Got let out on day parole and never went back."

"What did you — ?" Jesse began.

"Ever played baseball, Firelight?"

He gave me a puzzled look. "Three strikes and you're out," I said. "You just had your three."

For a minute Jesse just stared at me. Then he grinned. "Get out of here, city boy," he said, spreading out his books and papers on the table. "I've got work to do. Go hunt up your rodent and converse with somebody on a compatible intellectual level."

Eleven

Jesse was right about the cow penicillin. I didn't grow hoofs or horns or take up pawing the ground but I did get healthy real fast. I was out fencing with Jesse again when Carl and Connie rode up the next week. We had started feeding the cows every day so most of the herd showed up for breakfast. That gave Carl and Connie a chance to get a close look at some of them for the first time since June when they were trailed out here to the lease.

We rode through the cattle slow and easy with all three of the others making comments now and then when they spotted some cow that they knew by name. Not being personally acquainted with any of the ladies I kept quiet and listened. The names themselves were interesting enough. All the way from Old Obnoxious and Little Nasty to a mean-looking long-horned critter called Camaro. Something told me Jesse had named her.

All of a sudden Connie stopped her horse. "Carl! Look at Peggy Sue!"

We all reined in and looked at her. I didn't know which

one I was supposed to be looking at so I just looked. Carl did, though. "Hmm," he said, pushing back his hat.

"Hmm, nothing," said Connie disgustedly. "That little devil has gone and got herself pregnant."

"Does kind of look like it, doesn't it?" Carl agreed.

I didn't want to advertise my ignorance but I had the definite feeling I'd missed something here. "Aren't all these cows *supposed* to be pregnant?" Raising calves was the name of the game as far as I knew.

Connie nodded. "Yeah, Steve, the *cows* are supposed to be. But Sue's just a calf herself, barely a year and a half old. She wasn't supposed to be in calf for another year."

Right then I figured out which critter they were talking about. A kind of blondish little number that was all belly and looked a lot like a barrel set on four legs. I shook my head. Yeah, Preggy Sue, there ain't gonna be no prom for you.

"So what's gonna happen to her?" I asked.

"Well," Carl said, "she won't be due till January at the earliest. By then the cattle will be down home and we'll have to keep a close watch on her. She might have to have a zipper."

"A what?"

Connie laughed. "A Cesarean. Vets do them all the time on heifers that are too small to deliver their calves the usual way. leaves a neat little scar that looks like a zipper down their flank."

"No kiddin'? You have to take them into a clinic where everything's all sterile?"

It was Carl's turn to laugh. "Not exactly. If you ask the vet that question he'll tell you a few horror stories about doing them out on the range in a blizzard in the middle of the night. And ninety percent of the time both the cow and calf come out just fine. Cows are pretty tough. Anyhow, the vet always pumps the cow full of penicillin afterwards to keep her from getting an infection. Great stuff that penicillin."

Jesse caught my eye, and winked. I felt a sudden need to turn the other way and cough.

It snowed a little again the next week and turned quite a bit colder. We started bedding the cattle with straw near the bale stack and most of them were sticking around. Jesse said if this weather kept up we'd be moving them home before long.

It was Thursday, two weeks after the blizzard, and Jesse had left at noon again. I fixed a broken plant on the corral and made sure there was an open place in the creek where the cows could drink. I was just coming back from that when I noticed a cow lying down in the willows away from the rest of the herd. Jesse had taught me to check on any cow off by herself. Cattle aren't generally loners. As I got closer I noticed two things and neither of them was good news. The critter was kind of blondish, a color I'd only noticed on one of these cows before. And she was lying stretched out on her side looking sick as a dog. Yeah, it was Preggy Sue, all right. And, a minute later I understood what was wrong with her.

Maybe it *was* still November, and maybe Carl *had* said not till January, but obviously Sue hadn't been listening. She was about to have her calf today. I tried to remember how calves were supposed to be born but it's hard to remember what you never really knew. I wished I'd paid more attention to what I was reading in *Common Ailments of the Cow*. When I worked at the Quarter Circle it hadn't been calving time. I guess I *had* seen a few calves born way back when Pop had the ranch. But not many. Pop had a bunch of hardy old Herefords that mostly just disappeared in the brush alone and came back the next day with a wobbly calf trailing behind them.

But I didn't think it was going to happen that way for

Sue. If her calf was going to be born alive I was going to have to do something to help. What, exactly, was another question. It would be dark before I could ride down to the ranch and bring back somebody who knew what they were doing. But maybe that was still the best idea. I took two steps toward the barn before I remembered. Carl and Connie had taken off to visit some friends in Montana for a couple of days. Jesse had left early to do the ranch chores on his way through today. That left just me.

Sue struggled heavily to her feet, turned around a couple of times, and flopped back down again. She stretched out on her side and I saw the muscles along her belly ripple and tense as she lay straining for a minute or two. Then, with a kind of a moan, she relaxed and lay panting with a hopeless expression in her rolled-back eyes.

Minutes passed, then she pushed again and this time a pair of tiny, pale hoofs and the tip of a pink nose emerged from her body. Suddenly, a long-buried memory surfaced. Yeah, calves were *supposed* to be born front feet and nose first. That much was going right, at least. But, as the heifer relaxed again, the nose and hoofs almost disappeared back inside her. Great. That definitely wasn't part of the plan. Now what? I paced, trying to warm my freezing feet and calm my jangled nerves. I could ride down to the ranch and phone the vet. But I didn't know if I should leave Sue alone.

Why did everything happen on Thursdays. Jesse Firelight, if you ever go and leave me alone again here I swear I'll shoot out your tires.

Well, I sure wasn't doing any good just standing here. The horses needed feeding and there was the night's wood to pack into the cabin. I might as well go do it — and hope some miracle occurred by the time I got back.

The chores took about an hour. No miracle. About the only change was it was pitch dark now and the calf's feet were out another inch or two. Sue seemed to have about given up pushing and was just lying there breathing hard and looking like she was planning to die any minute. I had to do something. I shone the flashlight around and found a baler twine hanging on the fence. Okay, that would have to do.

I positioned the flashlight on the ground, and took off my gloves. Gingerly, I looped one end of the twine around each of the calf's slimy ankles. Then I grabbed hold of it in the middle of the twine. "All right, Sue," I muttered grimly. "I can't do this by myself. You gotta at least try." It took Sue some time to digest that information. I knelt shivering on the frozen ground, waiting. Finally, I saw the heifer's belly muscles start to tense. This was it. Sue grunted and pushed. I pulled on the twine, trying to keep the tension on both hoofs equal. The calf slid forward an inch or two. "All right, Sue!" I whispered admiringly. "You can do it!"

Minutes passed. The only sound was the hoarse panting of the cow — and me. Then, Sue pushed again. I pulled again. Suddenly the calf's head popped out. Through a covering of semitransparent membrane I could see the calf blink its eyes and twitch its nostrils. It just might suffocate before it was even born. I tried to pull the membrane off its face but the stuff was tough and slippery. I grabbed my knife from my pocket and used it to tear the membrane from the calf's nose. The calf took a bubbling gasp of air. I looked down at my razor-sharp six-inch switchblade and started to laugh. If the guys in Vancouver could see me now.

Sue pushed again and I pulled with all my strength. This one would do it. The calf was sliding, sliding, neck, shoulders, rib cage — and then it stopped. Jammed like a rock at the hips. Sue gave a pitiful moo. The calf gasped for breath. A few minutes like this and it would be dead.

"Come on, cow!" I yelled, gasping for breath myself. "Don't you quit on me now!" Sue pushed again and I pulled. I pulled till the thin twine cut into my hands like wire and my nearly-healed arm started throbbing. But the calf didn't move. I loosened the tension on the twine and sat there in the snow feeling more helpless than ever before in my life. And cursing myself for messing with things I didn't understand. Maybe if I had just left Sue alone Jesse would have been back in time to handle this. Now I'd probably killed both Sue and the calf.

One thing for sure, now I'd gone this far there was no going back. Desperately, I tightened my grip on the twine and pulled again, at more of a downward angle this time. And, all of a sudden, I felt the resistance lessen, then let go completely. With a gush of fluid the calf slid out to lie limp and steaming in the freezing night.

I glanced over at Sue. She lay flat on her side, also unmoving. Great. I had killed them both. Then, as I shone the light on the heifer I saw that she was breathing at least. Okay. She could wait. The calf needed attention fast. He was lying stretched out, limp and wet as a dead fish. "Come on calf, don't just lie there. Breathe!" I grabbed him by the slimy front legs and rocked him back and forth, hoping this might be the cow-equivalent of artificial respiration. He gave a weak, burbling gasp like he was trying to breathe underwater.

That was it! He had something in his throat. He needed draining. I picked up his hind legs and held him head down over my knee for a few seconds. He snuffled and snorted and suddenly came out with a feeble, "M-a-a-a!"

All right! He was going to live.

But then he started to shiver. This was one cold night to come into this world soaking wet. I looked around for a handful of hay to dry him off with. That's when I noticed that Sue had tucked her legs under her and was lying there like a normal, healthy cow. With any luck she was going to be okay, too.

I started rubbing the calf's quivering sides with the hay. He bobbed his head up and down and gave a little snort. "Way to go, kid! Keep fightin'!" I kept rubbing. He kept twitching and snuffling. There was a noise behind me and I glanced back in time to catch the shadowy movement of Sue scrambling to her feet. She gave a low moo. "Yeah," I muttered. "You *could* show a little interest. Dryin' him off is supposed to be *your* job. Don't you have any maternal instincts?" Come to think of it, far back as I could remember, my mom had never seemed too crazy about me but I'd figured cows came naturally equipped with all the right instincts. I must have figured wrong. Sue just nosed at a wisp of hay, rounded it up with her long tongue, and ate it.

Well, if she didn't care one way or another there wasn't much point in sitting out here freezing to death any longer. The calf might as well be in the barn, out of the wind at least. I tried to gather him up in my arms but he was all legs and slipperiness and I almost dropped him.

Smooth move, Steve. Go through all this and then break his neck. I tried again. He was a lot heavier than he looked. This wasn't working. Well, there was one way to do it. I crouched down, took a deep breath, and flung his filthy little body over my shoulders, hind legs on one side of my neck, front legs on the other. That was better. At least I wasn't going to drop him now. I took a couple of steps — and stopped dead in my tracks. Why did my neck suddenly feel so nice and warm — and *wet?* No, he wouldn't . . .

But he definitely had. "Well you rotten, ungrateful . . ." I set him down fast. But not fast enough. I pulled my soaking collar away from my neck and stood there steaming — physically and mentally. But, the damage was already done. I didn't have much to lose by finishing the job. I bent over to pick the little sucker up again. But he was starting to come alive enough to put up a little struggle this time. He jerked his head up and gave a loud "W-A-A-A-H!" that sounded like he was being murdered.

"Aw, shut up," I muttered, throwing him over my shoulders and heading for the barn, not quite as proud of saving his life as I'd been a minute ago. I thought I caught a movement behind me out of the corner of my eye but I didn't turn around. Walking over the rough ground with a calf on my shoulders and a flashlight in my hand was taking all my concentration. The calf struggled again. "W-A-A-A-H!"

There was a thud of hoofs on frozen ground and I heard a WHOOF! right behind me. The next thing I knew a locomotive had hit me in the back pockets and sent me — and the calf sprawling onto the ground. Fortunately for the calf, he landed in a pile of hay. I landed in something else. The light had gone out but even in the dark the smell was clear enough. For a minute I just lay there, taking in the aroma and wondering if it was safe to move.

Finally I chanced sitting up. Nothing attacked me. I felt around for the flashlight, gave it a shake, and the light came back on. I shone it around. There, just a few feet away was Preggy — I mean, *Peggy* Sue — standing protectively over her calf, licking it and making happy little cow sounds at it as it tried to collect all four legs and have a shot at standing up. Sue spotted me and glared, red-eyed in my direction.

I'd never felt more unappreciated in my life.

Twelve

A few days later we moved the cattle home for the rest of the winter. I'd expected it to take some hard riding to get all those cattle out of the brush and on the trail for home. But it didn't turn out that way at all. Carl and Connie came up with a truck and we loaded up all the groceries we had left — except for a loaf of bread I accidentally-on-purpose left behind for The Rodent.

We also loaded General Custer onto the front seat beside Connie. General Custer was Peggy Sue's calf. Jesse had named him. He said that since the calf was blond and not too bright and I had brought him into the world it was only right to name him in honor of my distinguished ancestor. The General lay there with his head up and his ears twitching and led the troops just like any other general, from a safe and comfortable place.

Carl drove behind Connie in the other truck with a bale of hay on it. And the cows poured down the trail behind him, pushing and jostling and galloping to catch up. They were going home and they knew it. All that was left for

Jesse and me to do was follow along and shut the gates behind us.

The winter turned out full of surprises. The first one came as soon as we got back from the lease. When we unloaded the truck I gathered up my belongings — which by now consisted of a spare shirt and jeans, two extra pairs of socks and some clean underwear Jesse had bought me — and started toward the bunkhouse. But Carl stopped me. "Not worth heating the bunkhouse all winter for just the two of you," he said. "We got a couple of spare bedrooms in the house." So, I found myself living with the boss — make that bosses.

One cold Thursday afternoon in December Carl was at a stock growers' meeting in Calgary and, of course Jesse was gone wherever he always went on Thursdays. All the chores were done and it was starting to get dark so I was in the living room watching World Wide Wrestling and Connie was in the kitchen making pies.

"Steve!" Connie hollered over the riot that was taking place on the screen.

"Yeah, Connie?"

"You busy?"

Well, that called for a big-time value judgement. I was busy watching wrestling. And I was busy scratching Bear, Connie's big, hairy black cat who was sleeping beside me with all four feet in the air.

"Not really," I said, cautiously.

"Good. I need you to peel apples for me."

I knew I should have been busy. Real men don't peel apples.

"Steve?"

"On my way, Connie."

I sat in the kitchen and peeled apples. I wasn't real good at it. The knife was dull. Twice I caught my hand edging toward my pocket for my own knife. No. Switchblades and apples don't mix. When Connie noticed the peels were turning out about as thick as the slices I got an instant lesson in apple peeling. "Took me a while to get Jesse trained for this, too," she said with a grin.

I couldn't help grinning back. Somehow the thought of old cool Jess getting drafted for apple peeling, too — and being lousy at it — made me feel real good. And, since Connie had brought up the subject of Jesse I figured now was my chance to ask a question that had been on my mind for a long time. "Connie, what's this Indian business Jesse does every Thursday anyhow?"

Connie stared at me like I'd lost my mind. "Indian business?"

I shrugged. "Yeah, that's what he said when I asked him where he was going the first Thursday I was here. I figured he must be goin' to some big pow-wow out on the reservation or somethin'."

All of a sudden Connie started to laugh. She laughed so hard she had to quit rolling her pie crust. Finally she got her breath back enough to talk. "Not exactly, Steve," she said, her voice threatening to dissolve into laughter again. "Jesse was pulling your leg. On Thursdays he goes to Calgary. To the university. He's working on his master's degree in environmental science."

I dropped the apple I was peeling. It rolled under the table and Bear woke up, came barrelling in and "killed" it instantly. It was a good thing The Rodent didn't live in this house.

I sat staring at Connie as a whole lot of little pieces started fitting together. All the time he spent studying those books. His reaction to what was going to happen to the Wolfsong Valley.

Connie gave me a curious look. "You and Jesse didn't find out much about each other in all that time alone out on the lease, did you?"

I figured that Jesse had found out way too much about me but all I said was "Jesse's not real big on talking about himself."

Connie smiled. "You're right about that." She hesitated a minute and then suddenly wiped her floury hands on her apron and poured two cups of coffee. She sat down and slid one across the table to me. "Maybe I've got no right to go telling tales out of school but there are some things I think you should know about Jesse.

"It was Christmas Eve, oh, seven, or eight years ago, when Carl and I first met Jesse. We didn't exactly meet him; we just barely missed running over him. We were on our way to visit friends in Calgary and it was a nasty, stormy night with visibility so bad we were about ready to give up and turn back. All of a sudden we spotted this figure staggering down the middle of the highway. Carl managed to swerve enough to miss him and then we stopped to see what was the matter. Here was this sixteen-year-old kid, wearing just a denim jacket, half-frozen to death, and too drunk to know it.

"He wouldn't tell us where he came from or where he was going and we sure couldn't just turn him loose again so we finally decided that there was only one thing to do. We turned around and took him home with us."

Connie shook her head and grinned ruefully. "And for a long time we wondered why. It was like trying to live with a young wildcat in the house. Jesse hated the whole world, including us, it seemed."

Connie poured more coffee, took a couple of pies out of the oven and stuck a couple more in. "It took a while," she continued, "and we came close to giving up more than once but gradually we found out the story behind Jesse Firelight.

"His family lived on a reserve near Calgary. He was in grade eleven, a top student and a pretty good hockey player. One November night his team was supposed to be playing in Calgary but a bad snowstorm came up and his dad told him not to go. But," Connie said with a sigh and a tired smile, "I don't have to tell you how pigheaded sixteen can be. Jesse took off and went anyway. Then his parents decided that if Jesse was determined to pay they had better drive in too and make sure he was okay." Connie sipped her coffee. "Well, to make a long story short Jessie made it to the arena all right. But his parents' car hit a snowplow. Both of them — and his two younger brothers — were killed instantly. Of course, Jessie blamed himself and the guilt almost killed him."

I studied the dark depths of my coffee, seeing Tracey's face, and remembering. "Yeah. Guilt can do that."

Connie went on. "By the time we inherited him Jesse was out of school, had run away from two foster homes, and was well on the way to being a teenage alcoholic."

"And now he's goin' for a master's degree at university? You and Carl must have done some kind of job of straightening him out."

Connie laughed. "Not really. I never did understand how it happened. By spring Carl and I were just about at the end of our rope with Jesse and he was getting angrier and more defiant every day. Then, one day he disappeared. We almost went out of our heads with worry, even reported him to the police as a missing person but they looked at his history and assured us he'd just run away again. That the streets were full of runaway kids and there was nothing anybody could do about it."

"They were right about that," I said quietly. Connie gave me a long questioning look but I concentrated on my coffee again.

She went on with her story. "I never really did believe he'd run away. I kept thinking something terrible had happened to him. And then about a week after he disappeared he walked in one night at supper time, exhausted, filthy, starved — but somehow at peace with himself. Just like that he announced he was going back to school. He did, too, caught up all he'd missed in no time, and became the best ranch hand we ever hired. But I don't think Carl and I can take the credit for turning Jesse around.

"I think the land straightened Jesse out. Just being here, close to the mountains, working with animals, being a part of the changing seasons. Jesse started to remember the things that mattered to him. Nature has a way of healing wounds, Steve. All we did was give him a place to live and enough hard work to sweat the anger out."

"Maybe that was all he needed." That, and the Wolfsong Valley I added silently. Connie stacked the cups in the sink and went back to rolling pie crust. I took the hint and started butchering another apple. All of a sudden I stopped and looked up at Connie again. "Does environmental science only have one class a week?" I asked, thinking that if that's how university operated maybe I should have skipped right there from junior high and missed a whole lot of hassle.

Connie smiled and shook her head. "One class at a time is all Jesse can afford. Or, at least the way he insists on going about things it is. There's all sorts of financial assistance available for students but Jesse won't touch a dime. Won't let Carl and me help him either. He's got too much pride for that. Going to do it all by himself or not at all."

"Stubborn, ain't he?"

Connie laughed. "There's a lot of that going around on the Double C."

I decided to let that one go by. "So, you think Jesse can do anything to stop them from clear-cutting his valley?"

Connie stopped the rolling pin in midstroke and looked

at me. "Jesse told you about the valley?"

"He showed it to me."

Connie's eyes widened a little. "Then I take it back," she said with a smile. "About you two not getting close alone out there on the lease for so long. If Jesse showed you the valley he must consider you a pretty good friend."

I wondered about that. Were Jesse and I friends? He'd saved my life. That was something you never forgot. But did it make us friends? Friends trusted each other . . .

"You didn't answer my question," I said. "About the valley."

Connie held out her hand for the bowl of apples I was just finishing. "Slowest apple peeler I ever trained," she muttered. Then she looked up and met my eyes. "I can tell you one thing, Steve. That project won't go ahead without a fight. I know of at least four environmental groups that are protesting it and I think Jesse's working for every one of them. He's spent every spare minute for the last six months researching and writing letters, helping set up court challenges, you name it."

"Has he got a chance to win?"

Connie sighed and brushed a hand across her forehead, leaving behind a streak of flour. She shook her head. "Just between you and me, Steve, I doubt it. I think it can be delayed while the government goes through all the right motions, environmental impact studies, all that jargon. But when it comes right down to it, the way the economy is these days there's no way they'll pass up a project that will provide that many jobs and that much tax revenue."

"So what does Jesse do when he runs out of legal ways to fight? Go for the illegal ones?"

I could almost see the color drain out of Connie's face. "I hope not," she said in a hushed voice.

Thirteen

December crawled on, dark and cold and slow. Ranch work slowed down to a crawl, too. I told Carl one day that I felt guilty getting paid for a day's work when mostly we just did a few hours chores and then holed up in the house for the rest of the day. He laughed. "Wait till calving times comes," he said. "That's when I get even. There won't be any overtime pay for those twenty-five-hour days you'll put in then."

But, while they lasted those winter days were some of the most peaceful of my life. The hard honest work in the biting cold and then the hours spent around the fire, playing crib with Carl or learning how to braid rawhide with Jesse. And Connie teaching me to cook — whether I wanted to learn or not. The outside world seemed a million miles away and I sometimes felt like this was what was real and my old life had just been some kind of bad dream. But once in a while something would happen to snap me back to reality. Like the night I looked up from my braiding to catch a glimpse of flashing red and blue lights coming down the lane. "Now what?" Carl muttered, going to open the door. Connie and Jesse stood up to get a better look out the window but I froze like a jack-lighted deer. I heard Carl talking to someone, then, "Steve! Come out here a minute, will you?"

This was it. I was trapped. I couldn't run. I couldn't fight. Not here in Carl and Connie's house. Feeling a big hollow space where my heart should be, I slowly walked toward the door. Carl stepped back. "Here he is, Sam," he said cheerfully to the Fish and Wildlife Officer who was waiting by the door, his truck sitting flashing its party lights outside. "Sam's on the trail of a deer poacher, Steve. You see anything suspicious when you got those bales off the west quarter just before dark?"

I took a couple of deep breaths so my voice wouldn't shake. "No, sir," I said. "But if I see any hunters I'll report them right away." And I meant it. Once you've been hunted you see hunting in a whole new light.

That incident broke the spell of peace and made me start thinking too much again. Thinking about what I was doing here, the things I'd done to wind up here, and what I was going to do come spring. And Christmas coming up didn't make me feel any better. I hadn't had too many good Christmases since I ran away. Sometimes, back in Vancouver, in the rain, I'd see a Christmas card with a picture of snow and spruce trees and people riding around in sleighs with horses and all that stuff and I'd get real homesick for Alberta. Not that any of my Alberta Christmases when I was a kid were exactly like the Christmas cards either. I wondered if anybody else's were either. Maybe that's why so many people are unhappy at Christmas. They're all expecting some kind of magic that never happens.

Christmas made me think about home. About Pop and Beau and how I hadn't spent a Christmas with them since I was twelve years old. And I thought about Raine a lot, too. About how she'd been my brother's girlfriend until I showed up. I wondered if I'd told Beau the truth when I said that I was seeing Tracey in Raine, that I didn't really love Raine. I decided that *was* the truth — mostly. Raine would always be someone real special to me but she'd always be Beau's girl, . . .

I was lying on my bed thinking about all that on Christmas Eve — and also thinking how lucky I was to have landed at a place like Johanneson's and feeling guilty because I didn't deserve to be treated so good — when there was a knock on the door. "Come in," I hollered and in walked Connie, wearing a dress. That startled me so much I sat up. She hadn't said anything about going out and Connie wasn't into getting dressed up for nothing.

I gave a low whistle just to annoy her a little. "Nice outfit, Connie. What's goin' on?"

A little grin almost escaped her before she remembered to look mad. "Mind your manners, child. I'd hate to have to smack you on Christmas Eve. Besides, I came to invite you out."

"Out?" I didn't go *out*. The farthest I'd been since coming here was to town to buy clothes and even that had me more nervous than a canary at a cat convention.

"Yes, *out* you hermit. To church. Christmas Eve service. Carl and I have been going for as long as I can remember. Jesse's coming and I was hoping you'd like to join us. How about it?"

I stared at her, completely stunned. *Church?* I hadn't been inside a church since Beau and me were little kids in Sunday school. I couldn't go to church.

"Well, Steve?"

"Uh, thanks Connie, but I, uh, don't have any church clothes."

She just laughed. "Come on, Steve, you can do better than that. Jesus was born in a stable, not the Bethlehem

Hilton. Those jeans are clean. You'll pass."

I shook my head. "I don't think I want to go, Connie."

Connie looked disappointed but she didn't push it. "Okay, Steve, it's up to you. But we won't be leaving for fifteen minutes so there's still time if you happen to change your mind."

The door closed behind her and I breathed a sigh of relief. No way was I about to change my mind. Suddenly the door opened again. No knock this time. Just Jesse, wearing a white shirt, a new pair of jeans, and a disapproving look. "Hey," he said, "aren't you coming?"

I shook my head. "I can't."

He walked over to the closet, pulled out my one decent shirt and my jacket, and threw them at me. "Move it, city boy. Connie wants you to come, you come."

Before I could answer he was on his way out the door. Halfway through he stopped and shot me a look over his shoulder. "Relax, Steve," he said with a hint of a grin. "Church is the last place you're likely to run into anybody who knows you."

The night was warm for December. A chinook had roared in across the mountains a couple of days back but now the wind was gone, leaving the foothills washed in a sea of soft, warm air. A few million stars spilled silver light into the darkness and, as we walked across the churchyard, a solitary coyote sang to the full moon. I wished I was out there in the hills with him. But, with Connie on one side, Carl on the other, and Jesse at my heels like an overeager cattle dog, there was no escape.

Next thing I knew we were inside the little white church. I breathed a sigh of relief when I saw that the only light came from the flickering candles along the walls and the colored lights on the big Christmas tree in one corner. It always felt safer in the shadows.

Connie and Carl and Jesse said Merry Christmas to a few people and shook hands with the preacher. Carl introduced me to him. "Hi, Steve. Glad you could come," he said, real easy. He didn't seem to notice I didn't belong. Maybe I wasn't wearing a sign with two-inch letters saying WANTED DEAD OR ALIVE after all.

We sat down and I finally started to relax enough to pay attention to what was going on. The service started with some Christmas carols. I couldn't remember the last time I'd heard Christmas carols when I wasn't in a shopping mall. They sounded a lot different with real live people singing.

After the singing the preacher read the Christmas story while some little kids acted it out with real animals. Sheep, goats, a Holstein calf — and a miniature donkey that let go with a full-grown bray right in the middle of the prayer. The kid who was holding him turned so red I thought he was going to have a meltdown right there.

I looked at those little kids' faces and wondered what it would be like to be that young and innocent again. I wondered if I ever *had* been that young and innocent.

The story ended. "Glory to God in the highest and on earth, peace, goodwill to men," the preacher said.

Good luck, I thought bitterly. Have you looked around the real world lately, Reverend? For a couple of thousand years people have been reading all that peace and good-will stuff but it ain't happened yet — and it never will.

Then the organ was playing "Silent Night" and the congregation was singing. I watched Carl and Connie as their calm, lined, and weather-beaten faces caught the glow of the candlelight. And, suddenly, I realized I was wrong. There *was* peace on earth — if you knew where to look for it. It was here, on the faces of honest, hard-working, decent people. The kind of people who would take in a drunk Indian kid on Christmas Eve or invent a job for a broke drifter who might rob them blind or murder them in their beds for all they knew.

For a few candlelit minutes there, even I knew what peace felt like.

But, on Christmas Day something came up that made my life less peaceful and a whole lot more complicated. It started out harmless enough. We were all sitting around digging into the biggest turkey dinner I'd ever seen assembled at one table when Jesse made some comment about something he'd learned at university once. That led to some more discussion about university courses and then all of a sudden, right out of the blue, Connie said, "Have you ever thought of going to university, Steve?"

I laughed. "I don't think the university would be too impressed with my grade-six education."

Connie passed me the sweet potatoes. "Come on, Steve. It can't be *that* bad. How far did you *really* get in school?"

I swallowed a mouthful and looked up at her. "I ain't kiddin'. I only made it halfway through grade seven."

Carl set down his fork and gave me a skeptical look. "Well, I know that sort of thing happened all the time when I was a kid. But things are different now. Didn't the authorities track you down when they found out you weren't going to school?"

I shrugged. "They might of tried. But I wasn't around to find out. The day after I got suspended I hitched a ride to Vancouver and disappeared. My dad didn't even know where I was."

Suddenly I noticed everybody had stopped eating and were sitting there waiting expectantly for the next chapter of this story. I couldn't believe I'd even been stupid enough to tell them chapter one. And I sure wasn't about to tell them any more. I looked down at my plate and concentrated on shoveling in the grub. Gradually, other knives and forks began to clink again. I breathed a sigh of relief — too soon.

"That's all the more reason you need to think about getting yourself some more education before it's too late, Steve." Connie sounded concerned. "You can't make a decent living without at least a high school education."

I gave her a dirty look, mostly because she was dead right and I hate it when people are right about me. I'd already tried most of the things you can do without an education. Ninety percent of them were illegal. The rest were mainly dirty, dangerous, and paid about enough to eat once a week if you were lucky. "It's already too late."

"Why?"

The woman was harder to shake loose than a determined pit bull. "I don't exactly fit those junior high desks anymore," I said with a grin.

Before Connie could think of an answer to that one good old Jesse landed in the middle of the conversation. "How old are you, Steve?"

"None of your business," was the most polite answer that flashed through my mind but this *was* Christmas so I just glared at him and muttered, "Nineteen."

"Then, although we'd never know it," his mouth twitched at the corners, "you're an adult. You can go back to school as an adult student and they won't make you go back where you left off. You can start in high school."

I laughed. "Yeah, Jess, sure I can. Except that I happen to have a job here for the rest of the winter, remember?"

There was a moment's silence in which I optimistically assumed we'd finished that subject and got on with eating my turkey. Wrong again.

Connie looked thoughtful and then said, "Second semester doesn't start till February, does it Jesse?"

"Nope."

"Well, we've got to have someone on night shift

during calving so we could put Steve on then and he could go to school during the day, couldn't he, Carl?"

"Don't see why not."

"Yeah? And when am I supposed to sleep?"

Carl grinned. "Young guys like you don't need sleep."

I looked around at the three of them, all happy as could be at reorganizing my life. I seemed to be the only one there who didn't have anything to say. I put down my fork, pushed back my chair, and said, real slow and clear so none of them could miss it, "I ain't goin' back to school. Period. Case closed."

Jesse pushed back his chair. "Don't have the guts to try it, do you, city boy?"

Fourteen

*O*n February second I drove into the school parking lot. Sneaked in was more like it. I was driving Jesse's truck, which had to be one of the all-time most humiliating experiences of my life. And I had a feeling this episode was going to get a lot more humiliating before it was over. Mentally I cursed Jesse Firelight for backing me into this corner. Saying I didn't have the guts to do this. I had guts enough to do anything — *except* this, I thought, getting an overwhelming desire to turn around and get out of here while I still could. I probably would have done it, too, except that Connie had offered to come with me to register and I had the feeling that if I didn't do it alone today she *would* come with me tomorrow.

Walking into the school felt eerily the same as when I was escorted into prison last year. Trapped. I tried to ignore the stares from the kids in the hall. I didn't figure I looked all that conspicuous. I had on faded jeans, sneakers, a sweat shirt, and down jacket. (The jacket was Jesse's. My one and only jacket had taken on a strong aroma of cow the night before when I was trying to teach the world's stupidest calf how to suck.) Most of the other guys were wearing basically the same things — except for the really cool dudes who had on their flowered pajama bottoms or something. And even if I was technically an adult I was less than a year older than most of the grade twelves here so I didn't think I was standing out like a senior citizen or something. It was probably because it was a real small town and *any* stranger was worth staring at — either that or I was wearing that WANTED DEAD OR ALIVE sign again.

I went into the office, told the secretary what I wanted and got handed a form to fill out. It was three pages long. Geez, lady, if I could understand all this I wouldn't *need* any more education. I sighed, sat down and did the best I could. Some of the stuff I could answer honestly — like when I was born. After that, I had to get a little more creative. But, I finally finished it and gave it back to the secretary. She took it into the principal's office and came back and told me he'd see me in a minute. I sat down — and waited twenty minutes. Then her intercom beeped. She answered it and then nodded to me. "Mr. Waters will see you now."

I walked in and stood in front of the desk while a balding guy with glasses sat there studying my registration form and ignoring me completely. I shifted restlessly, wondering if there was still time to make a run for the door. Finally the principal gave a sigh like a horse that's been clinched up too tight and looked up at me. "You're Steve Bonney?"

I nodded.

"Last grade completed, *seven?*" he read, wrinkling his forehead like he was having trouble with his eyesight. "Is this correct?"

I hesitated. "Well, not exactly."

Mr. Waters looked relieved. "Thank heaven! And

what *should* this say?"

I tried to think of the best way to put this. There wasn't one. "I, uh, guess it should say attended, not completed."

Mr. Waters rubbed his forehead. "Go on," he said in a low voice.

"Well, I didn't actually *finish* grade seven."

The principal's frown deepened. "I see. And what, may I ask, motivated you to leave school in grade seven?"

I thought that one over. "The principal, mainly."

If Waters had been a dog, I think the hair along his back would have stood up. "I beg your pardon?" he growled.

"He was the one that kicked me out," I said.

There was a real long silence. At last the principal adjusted his glasses and gave me a cold look. "I might as well tell you right now that I have serious reservations about you. The law says I have to accept people like you who want to come back and have a belated try at making something of themselves. But," he added, his glasses glinting so I couldn't see his eyes, "that doesn't mean I have to like it."

Yeah, I thought, and the facts of life say I have to accept people like you if I want to get enough education to survive in this world, but that doesn't mean I have to like it either.

Waters stood up. "So, uh," he'd already forgotten my name, "Steve, what I'm telling you is walk softly in my school. I'll be watching you."

Great. I stay away from school for seven years, come back, and I'm right back where I started, branded bad and marked for trouble. But I took a deep breath and said, "Yes sir," just like a properly housebroke student.

"All right then, go on into the guidance office and Ms. Lafontaine will set up your schedule."

Ms. Lafontaine was just the opposite of Mr. Waters and I didn't like her much better. She was so busy polishing up my self-image I was afraid she'd wear it out before I got out of there. Oh sure, I could handle high school courses. No doubt about it. Too bad I had to work as well, though. She hoped my job wouldn't interfere with my schoolwork. I didn't have the heart to tell her that I just hoped my schoolwork didn't interfere with my job. She plugged me into two classes, English and social studies, which she said were pretty basic to getting any kind of a diploma. "Come on," she said, "your English class has already started. I'll take you down and introduce you to Ms. Tremayne."

We walked down the long, empty hall and stopped in front of Room 18. The door was closed. Ms. Lafontaine knocked. And I panicked. Because it suddenly hit me just how far out of my territory I really was. There wasn't a dark street in Vancouver I was scared to walk down, a waterfront hood I wouldn't fight if I thought he needed it, or a bad bronc I wouldn't climb on just to see if I could ride him, but this was different. Seven years ago I'd been flunking grade seven. Now I was just about to walk into a high school class and pretend I knew what I was doing. I spotted a big EXIT sign at the end of the hall. But, before I could do anything about it, the door opened. Ms. Tremayne, I presumed.

Ms. Tremayne was young — a whole lot younger than they'd been making English teachers last time I was in school. Her blond-streaked light-brown hair was done up in a long braid, and she was wearing a white blouse and a denim skirt. The only other thing I noticed about her at that moment was that she was looking at me like I was a well-rotted gopher her dog had just dragged in. I wondered what somebody had done to her corn flakes this morning. "Yes?" she said coolly.

"We have another student for you, Ms. Tremayne," Ms. Lafontaine chirped.

"You've got to be kidding!" Ms. Tremayne blurted out and then she must have noticed that wasn't a real teacherish thing to say because she suddenly turned red and stammered, "I, uh, mean I've already got thirty-seven kids crammed in here. They're practically hanging out the windows as it is. I haven't got a single extra desk," she added hopefully like it would mean she couldn't possibly let me in.

Ms. Lafontaine smiled the kind of understanding smile of a person who doesn't actually have to live with a situation. "Lynne, I know the overcrowding this semester is just insane. But the janitor told me he stacked some spare desks outside the library so at least that problem's solved." She turned to me, "Good luck, Steve. You can do it. Just keep thinking that. Put yourself in a position of power and you can conquer anything." I stared after her as she sailed off down the hall wondering if she got that philosophy from Saddam Hussein. I turned to look at Ms. Tremayne. She hadn't cheered up one bit. Maybe Ms. Lafontaine should have given her some words of wisdom, too. She looked distractedly over her shoulder. The noise level in the room behind her had gradually risen to a dull roar.

"Sit *down*, Harold," she ordered. "Settle down, Ruth and Dolores." Suddenly a badly engineered paper airplane made a nose-first landing by the door. She reached down, picked it up, and smoothed it out. "Artie," she sounded real tired, "if you *must* turn your course outline into an airplane it would be a whole lot smarter not to put your name on it so you could blame someone else." She refolded it and sailed it back to a grinning kid in the back row. "Now get that smoothed out and into your notebook where it belongs before I sail *you* out of this class. One less body in this room wouldn't break my heart."

She turned back to me. "Okay, Steve," she said wearily, "Come on in. Welcome to English 23."

The room was hot and stuffy with wall-to-wall bored people. And there I was, a brand-new tourist attraction. Instantly thirty-seven sets of eyeballs homed in on me like radar. I couldn't handle this. But before I could say, "Beam me up, Scottie," Ms. Tremayne took control, "Class," she said, not real enthusiastically, "this is Steve Bonney."

"Hi Bonnie!" a heavyset redheaded guy in the back hollered and about six other guys laughed hysterically.

"H-e-y! He's cute!" an overgrown blonde whose family must have owned the hairspray concession said in a whisper designed to carry to the front of the room.

I gave them all a cold stare.

"Ron," said Ms. Tremayne.

A big, round-faced guy who'd been reclining peacefully in a front desk jumped. "Huh?"

Ms. Tremayne sighed. "Try 'pardon me,' Ron. Go and help Steve find a spare desk down by the library, please."

Ron yawned and stretched. "I guess so," he said and lumbered out of his desk and down the hall. Gratefully, I followed.

We found the desks and headed back to the room. Halfway back Ron asked, "Got a smoke?"

"No" I said. We ran out of things to talk about. We put the desk in the only space there was — about six inches away from the teacher's desk. I doubted that Ms. Tremayne was going to enjoy that any more than I was. I took one last glance back at the class as I sat down. So these were the good guys, the ones who were in school, getting an education and making something of themselves.

I was starting to get real homesick for the intelligent face of a cow.

Fifteen

*T*he first thing I learned was that I had a lot to learn. And not just the stuff you got from books. I had to learn about reading teachers and playing the system and all the other stuff that every other high school kid had already figured out. For one thing, my two classes were so different I couldn't believe they took place on the same planet. Mr. Melnychuk, my social studies teacher, was a facts man. He told us about the natural resources of the Yukon and the causes of World War II and anything else the course of studies said we needed to know and all we were expected to do was to write it down and cough it up again when the exam came around. It was more boring than picking hayseed out of your socks but it was safe. Jump through the hoops, you pass the course.

But that wasn't how Ms. Tremayne operated. She announced the first day that there would be no such thing as a multiple-guess test in her class. As far as she was concerned, an English class meant just that. English. We were going to write it, read it, and speak it until we got it right. She sent us home with a twenty-page short story to read and write our impressions of that first night. My first impression was that whoever said twenty pages was *short* should be sued for false advertising.

For once I was ready to join Jesse with my head buried in a book all evening. I figured I might even be able to get him to tell me what my impressions of the story were but, as it turned out, he wasn't even home that evening. Come to think of it, he was hardly ever home these evenings. He didn't talk about it much but I knew from what Connie said that he was out at meetings about the valley. There was a big public hearing coming up in a couple of months to decide whether the whole project could go ahead or not and I guess he was doing everything he could to get ready for it.

It was after midnight by the time I got the homework done. Reading the story hadn't been so bad but when it came to writing about it I had to look up about every fourth word in the dictionary to find out how to spell it. As far back in school as I can remember teachers were always saying, "Look it up if you can't spell it." I never did figure out how you were supposed to find a word in the dictionary if you couldn't spell it in the first place.

When I finally packed up the books and fell into bed I was still thinking about the story I'd read, school in general, and Ms. Tremayne. The ghosts weren't coming around as much these nights. But I knew they weren't gone for good, Tracey's face would be back. And the nightmare of Romero would never die — until he did.

The next morning I was sleepily shoveling in breakfast when Connie glanced out the window. "Oh, shoot! The cows are in the hay corral!" Sure enough, they'd broken through the fence and the whole couple hundred of them were doing a search-and-destroy mission through the bale stacks. All four of us threw on our jackets and tore out of the house.

By the time we had the cattle chased out I was already late for school so I left the others to fix the fence, jumped in Jesse's truck and roared out of there as fast as it could limp.

I was right. I *was* late for school. So I got to make my second grand entrance into English class. Ms. Tremayne was not impressed. When I knocked she flung the door open so I almost fell into the classroom. "Late again, Steve?" she said icily.

"Yeah, Bonnie!" yelled the redhead in the back whose name was Mitch. The whole class cheered. Ms. Tremayne gave them a teacher look that was supposed to crack faces but nobody disintegrated. She went back to what she'd been doing when I came in. Collecting homework. "Jeff?" she said.

"I forgot my book at school," a little guy with glasses said. "I'll do it tonight."

"Mary Ann?"

"I couldn't do mine. I had to babysit."

"Barbara?" She handed hers in.

"Mike?"

"Mine's in my dad's car in Calgary."

The list went on. I think there were six people who actually handed their work in. At least another six were absent. Ms. Tremayne got to the last guy in the alphabet.

"Mitch?"

The redhead propped his chin up on one elbow like he was having trouble keeping awake. "Forgot it at home," he said, his voice bored.

That did it. Ms. Tremayne twisted right off. "You *forgot* it!" she echoed. "You left yours in the car! You had to babysit!" Her eyes flashed angrily around the room and for the first time I noticed they were brown. Kind of a pretty brown. "What do you people think I'm running here? Daycare? If you don't care enough to do the work, why are you even in school? I'll tell you one thing for sure, if only the people who were here with the faintest intention of learning something stayed, there'd be no more overcrowding problem. You make me sick, all of you."

Wow! She was good. The room was eerily silent for a few seconds — the first time it had been quiet so far. Then, Ms. Tremayne's gaze fell on me. "Oh, yes, and the late, great Mr. Bonney. May I have your homework, please?"

And right then I got a very clear picture in my mind. My three hours' worth of neatly written homework lying on the chair by the kitchen door, right where I left it so I couldn't miss it when I left for school.

I sighed. Ms. Tremayne shifted restlessly. "Your *homework*, Steve."

"I forgot it at home," I said.

The tension in the class suddenly dissolved as the whole room exploded in laughter. Ms. Tremayne tossed back a strand of hair that had escaped from her braid. "Right, Steve," she said, her eyes burning the word "liar" into my face. "I'll say this for you. You catch on fast."

I met her eyes. "Not fast enough," I said. I got up and walked out of the room. A stunned silence followed me out the door.

On my first couple of trips to town I'd been so worried about attracting a cop I'd been driving like somebody's grandpa. That was about to change. Jesse's truck had more speed in it than I would have ever believed. If it had been a horse it would have dropped dead as I pulled up in front of the kitchen door. I charged into the house, picked up my notebook, and was halfway out the door before Connie could look up from the dishes she was washing and say, "Wha . . . ?"

She may have said more but it was drowned in the roar

of the truck starting again. The trip back to town took two minutes less than the trip out. I ran all the way from the parking lot into the school but I was still too late. English period had been over for three minutes. I tried the classroom door. It was locked. My temper exploded. I kicked the door so hard it rattled in its frame. All of a sudden the door was jerked open. Ms. Tremayne stood there, her face white with fury. "You! What do you think . . ."

I slapped my notebook into her hand. "Here's my homework."

She opened her mouth to say something, stopped, glanced down and opened the book, riffled a few pages, and then looked up at me again. "You really did have it done," she said, quietly.

"Yeah, I really did."

"How far did you drive to get this?"

I shrugged. "Forty miles, give or take."

"Just to prove I was wrong about you?"

I shook my head. "No, maybe to prove I was right about me."

There was a silence. When Ms. Tremayne spoke again her voice was kind of hoarse, like maybe she was having a little trouble getting the words out. "I'm sorry, Steve."

"Me, too," I said, and turned and walked away. I didn't know what I was sorry for. Maybe that I didn't hate her as much as I had planned to.

From then on, things were different between Ms. Tremayne and me. I did all my work, kept my mouth shut in class, and stayed out of trouble. And once in a while I'd look up from my work and catch her watching me. The look that passed between us then, was it respect, or something more?

Calving started and a spell of cold weather hit at the same time, and I learned that Carl hadn't been lying about those twenty-five-hour days. Every afternoon just before dusk we'd check all the cows, look them over, and take bets on which ones would calve before morning. Then we'd cut those out and put them in the barn for the night. Then, as darkness set in and the temperature started edging down past thirty below, we all took turns going out to check on the ones outside, watching for the ones we'd guessed wrong about. There were always some that fooled us and we'd end up carrying these cold, wet, slimy calves into the barn, trying to get them warmed up before they turned into Popsicles on us. Everybody got tired, frost-bitten, and sour. A couple of days I missed school completely but I still had almost the best attendance in class. And, I kept up with my homework — in my sleep sometimes — but I did it. Ms. Tremayne and I were still getting along, sort of. I'd got pass marks on all the assignments so far — just. I got comments like, "Shows thought," or "Interesting observation," on the answers I wrote to her questions on the stories we were reading and I usually got 10 or 12 out of 15 on that part but then there was always a section for grammar, punctuation, and spelling. Two out of five was my all-time record on that part.

If Mr. Waters was watching me like he'd promised, at least he was doing it from a distance. The closest we came to a conversation was when we'd pass in the hall and he gave me a dirty look. I discovered a few of the kids in class — the quiet ones — were okay. I could phone them for assignments I'd missed or sometimes study with them at lunch time. But I didn't really think of them as friends, the way I thought of Jesse. He was the best friend I'd ever had. Except for Tracey. Tracey had been my friend long before she was my girlfriend.

But I saw less and less of Jesse these days. Either I was at school or he was at a meeting or both of us had our heads buried too deep in the books to even talk to each other. One cold Friday afternoon he was gone to Calgary for a meeting with the environment minister. Jesse and some other guys were presenting some research paper they had worked on for months and it was supposed to convince the guy to block the valley project.

Jesse didn't make it home for supper. I figured no news was good news. If the meeting was taking this long the guy must at least be listening to them. But Jesse didn't make it home for cow check at ten o'clock, either.

At two, sure enough, there was a shivering little surprise steaming in the freezing dark. I got the calf inside all right but then spent the next half hour doing my own little Olympics trying to get its brainless mother to go into the barn with it. I had crawled back into bed and was curled up like a hibernating squirrel trying to get warm again when Jesse drove in. A couple of minutes later I heard the back door open and then footsteps on the stairs. I dragged myself out of bed and down to Jesse's room. He hadn't even turned the light on. "Hey, Jess," I said, keeping my voice low so I wouldn't wake up Carl and Connie. "How'd it go?" There was a long silence. "Jess?"

He swung around to face me in the darkness. "Guess," he said bitterly. And, for the first time since I'd known Jesse I knew he'd been drinking.

Sixteen

---

*J*esse didn't show up for breakfast the next morning. Carl and Connie didn't say much but I could see they were kind of worried about him. I don't know what happened during the day but by the time I got home he was out trying to teach a pair of dim-witted newborn twins which end of the cow produced the milk. He didn't say anything about last night and I didn't ask him but I couldn't help wondering what would happen if he lost the final round of the fight for his valley. He still thought he could win — or at least he was doing a pretty good job of convincing himself. He was already talking to Carl and Connie about some new strategy he was working on.

But, as the days passed and the deadline for the final decision on the valley got closer, Jesse got quieter, more alone. Whatever he was thinking, he kept it to himself. Sometimes it seemed like the longer I knew him, the less I *really* knew him. Until the day when I accidentally discovered something that gave me a whole new picture of Jesse Firelight.

A chinook had finally blown in and got us out of the

deep freeze. The calves were all out suntanning on the warm hillside behind the barn and Jesse and I were walking around them, checking for sick ones. There were always one or two that needed a shot of antibiotic or a pill or something. Sure enough, one calf was standing by the fence all humped up and staring miserably into space. Its nose was runny and its other end was runny and it definitely was not a happy calf.

Jesse looked it over. "Better get a shot of liquamycin into him right away." He took another look. "Looks like his navel could be infected, too. Run and get the iodine, will you Steve?"

"Sure." I started off toward the house. I was maybe a hundred yards away when something made me look back over my shoulder. Jesse was kneeling beside the calf, filling the syringe. All his attention was focused on the calf and the needle and he didn't notice that fate was bearing down on him from the opposite direction.

Snake-Eye, the old dog, had apparently just woke up and discovered we were gone so now he was walloping up through the herd of cattle headed for Jesse. That was starting to cause a commotion. All across the hillside, big mamas looked up from their breakfast and bawled worriedly as this deadly "wolf" galloped carelessly past their children.

Jesse had the needle ready. "Snake-Eye, you dumb dog," I heard him mutter as the dog panted up and slopped a big, wet kiss on his face just as he slid the needle into the calf's shoulder. The calf gave an injured "BAWP!" which instantly got its mother's attention. Its mother was Old Longhorn, the biggest, meanest, and, yeah, the longest-horned cow in the herd. I don't know exactly what passed through Longhorn's miniature mind at that moment but it obviously had something to do with Jesse, the dog, and the fact that, between them, they'd made her baby cry. She made a sound halfway between a bawl and a snort, lowered her head, and charged. Jesse was still looking down at the calf.

"Jesse!" I yelled, "Look out!" When you've been around cattle as long as Jesse has, you don't stand there saying, "Huh?" He dived for cover — right through the barbed wire fence. Longhorn skiddded to a stop beside her calf but still managed to hit the fence hard enough to make the wires squeal. The dog dived under the fence in time to escape with his life, wagged his tail, gave an excited yap at how much fun this all was, and trotted happily over to see if Jesse needed any first aid. I trotted back with the same thing on my mind.

Jesse was just getting up and wiping cow pasture souvenirs off his jeans. He looked over at Longhorn who was still standing over her calf with her eyes glowing faintly red. "Good, motherly cow," he said with a grin.

"Yeah," I said, "any better and you'd be dead. How'd you get through that fence in one piece?"

He laughed, shook his head, and said, "Pure terror!" He wiped his scratched hands on his jeans, then ran a hand across the torn shoulder of his denim jacket. He winced and his hand came away red. "Guess I didn't make it in one piece after all."

He left Longhorn in charge of the hillside and headed for the house. Carl and Connie were away so it was up to me to play doctor. "Okay, Jess," I smiled as I got out the bottle of antiseptic, "*my* turn."

Jesse poured two mugs of coffee and shook his head "Forget it, Steve. This is nothing."

"Too bad you ain't a white man," I said, reversing the line Jesse had used on me that night in the blizzard. I could see Jesse remembered it, too. "Why?" he said cautiously.

"'Cause a white man wouldn't be scared to let me

clean out a little cut with this good, powerful, stinging disinfectant," I said with an evil grin. "Stop feeling sorry for yourself. At least this stuff's made for people."

"You don't have to enjoy yourself quite so much," Jesse said sourly, but he unbuttoned his shirt and pulled it off his bleeding shoulder. The cut was messy — about two inches long and deep enough to have bled pretty good. I wet a rag and washed off the blood trailing from the top of his shoulder down over his collarbone to redden the feathers of the tattooed eagle that flew just below it. I studied the eagle. Something about that tattoo brought back a memory from somewhere.

"This some kind of a tribal symbol, Jess?" I picked a scrap of shirt out of the cut. Jesse shifted and I wasn't sure if it was because of my doctoring or my question.

I looked at him and waited for an answer. His eyes met mine for a second and then moved away to focus on something outside the window. "Guess you could say that," he said softly.

I sloshed some disinfectant into the cut. Jesse swore at me under his breath. I ignored him. "Yeah." I taped some gauze over the cut. "But you don't have to be an Indian to get one of those amateur tattoos, do you? I almost got one myself once." Jesse's eyes never left the faraway mountains but I felt his muscles tense a little. "Matter of fact," I went on, "I *did* one for another guy. Not an eagle, though. Mine was a real artistic marijuana leaf. You do them with a needle and thread and ballpoint ink, don't you Jesse? The guy I did it for was my cell mate." I stepped between Jesse and the window so he had to look at me. "That's a *prison* tattoo, ain't it, Jesse?"

Jesse just took a deep breath and sat there staring right through me, and that's when I got mad. "All right, Mr. Truth-and-Honesty, you were so all-fired insulted when you thought I wouldn't tell you the truth about me. Why don't *you* try tellin' me a little truth for a change. Who are you, Jesse?"

"You know who I am." Jesse's voice was expressionless.

"Right, Jess — if that really is your name. You keep changin' faster than a chameleon in a rainbow. One minute you're a dead-broke loser in a rusted-out truck, the next you're some big-time university graduate environmentalist. And now," I paused to give him a long, cold look and to make sure the words sunk in good and deep, "You're nothin' but an ex-con." I paused. "Like me."

Jesse didn't say anything.

"Well, Jess, what's the story?"

He stood up and paced around the room a couple of times and finally stopped and faced me. "All right, if you've got to know, I'll tell you." His voice was soft but his eyes were harder than I'd ever seen them. "You ever hear of a place called Oka?"

It didn't ring any bells right off. Then it all came back to me. I'd never paid much attention to the news but that one summer you could hardly *not* hear about Oka. "You mean down in Quebec where the Indians blocked the highway and stood off half the army all summer?"

Jesse nodded. "Yeah, that's the place." There was a silence and then, "I was one of the guys behind the barricades." There was no pride in his voice. There was no shame either as he added, "I did some time after it was all over."

I thought back, sifting through the hazy memories of the news stories, and the more I thought the more confused I got. None of the pieces fit together. Not with what Connie had told me. Had everything Jesse told her been a lie? "You mean you're really an Iroquois?" I said.

Jesse shook his head. "No, I'm Alberta born and raised. I was just stupid enough to go a couple of thousand miles east to get in the same kind of trouble I could've found in my own backyard. I'd just finished my fourth year of university in Calgary and I knew I wanted to get my master's degree in some kind of environmental studies. Eventually I wanted to write a thesis on something to do with the relationship between native land claims and preserving the environment. Then, when all the trouble broke out at Oka about destroying a forest the natives thought they owned in order to build a golf course I figured it was the best chance I'd ever get for a firsthand look at the subject."

"And you ended up having an eyeball-to-eyeball look at the army while you were at it?"

"Yeah. I was really young and full of big ideas about how we were going to change the world. I started listening to these warriors talk about how, just once, they were going to make someone listen and I started to believe it. I was really going to *do* something." He laughed bitterly. "And all I ended up *doing* was three months in prison." He buttoned his shirt and pulled on his jacket, his movements filled with the pent-up violence he'd been carrying a long time. "You feel better now you know?" he asked, his voice hard-edged.

I nodded. "Yeah, Jess, I do. You feel a lot worse now you told me?" Jesse didn't answer for a minute. Then a kind of sheepish grin crept across his face. "No," he muttered.

We went out to feed the cows.

Seventeen

Days and nights slid by. Sometimes it was hard to remember which was which when between homework and cow problems my head seemed to barely hit the pillow before the alarm clock was yelling in my ear again. One weekend I wound up getting a grand total of four hours' sleep. That was the time Carl and Jesse made what was supposed to be a day trip to Great Falls to pick up a new bull and got caught in a blizzard and had to stay for three days. The same blizzard hit us at the ranch, too, and Connie and I worked nonstop all day, putting cows in, moving others to where there was more shelter, putting out extra straw for bedding.

On Saturday night five calves were born. Three of them were to cows we'd guessed wrong about and left outside. One of the calves was so far gone Connie decided the only chance to save it was to bring it in, put it in a bathtub of warm water, and blow it dry with the hair dryer. And I thought *I* could mess up a bathtub. The calf survived but by the time he was lively enough to take back to his mother she thought he smelled all wrong and refused to let him anywhere near her. We had to hog-tie her before she'd let the calf suck.

At eleven o'clock Sunday night I fell asleep over my homework and Connie made me go to bed, saying she'd check the cows that night. At two-thirty Connie shook me awake. She'd found one of the heifers about to calve outside. We went out and put her into the barn. By then Connie was almost asleep on her feet so I sent her in. I huddled in the straw and waited. And waited. At last, the heifer produced a foot. I rubbed my eyes sleepily, hoping I wasn't seeing straight. But, I was. It was a *hind* foot. A really big hind foot. I groaned. A first-calf heifer with a really big, backward calf was all we needed at — I checked my watch — four-fifteen on Monday morning. I went to wake Connie.

She checked things out, shook her head, and headed back toward the house. "Time to support our local veterinarian," she said with a tired grin.

Ever since Carl had told me about how vets did Cesareans I'd been kind of curious about them. By six o'clock I wasn't curious anymore. Instead I was bloody to the elbows from helping to hold in all the parts that weren't supposed to fall out as the vet and Connie delivered the calf through the long slit in the side of the cow. Cows sure do have a lot of guts. Obviously, *Common Ailments of the Cow* had been right about cows having four stomachs — and every one of that heifer's stomachs had seemed about ready to land in my lap.

Amazingly, it all worked fine. In no time the heifer was happily licking a 110-pound bull calf that was already making energetic little noises and trying to stand up. The heifer and calf sure seemed to feel a lot better than I did.

I had just enough time to shower and gulp down three

cups of black coffee before I left for school. I wanted to stay home and help Connie but she said that since it had quit snowing and was warming up she could manage and I couldn't afford to miss class. You don't argue with Connie.

It was a typical Monday at school. About a quarter of the class was absent. Of the ones that were there I would have bet another quarter were still hung over from weekend parties. There wasn't a whole lot of enthusiasm in English class. Especially not for the novel we were supposed to be studying.

It was called *On the Beach* and no, it didn't have anything to do with girls in bikinis. But, it was kind of interesting. It took place in Australia after the rest of the world had just finished a big war and nuked itself out of existence. Australia hadn't even been damaged so the people were all fine — except the fallout was drifting slowly south and was going to kill them all in a few months. The book was all about the ways people reacted to the fact they were about to die. How they chose to spend their last few months of life.

I was sitting there with a pounding headache from not getting any sleep, listening to Ms. Tremayne talking about the book, and trying not to fall asleep. She was asking questions now. "Dennis, what do you think the author is trying to say about how the knowledge of certain death affects people?"

Dennis, who as far as I knew, had never spoken a word that didn't relate to the NHL, looked at her like she'd lost her mind. "I dunno," he muttered.

"Mary Ann, what do you think?"

Mary Ann shifted in her desk and studied her sneakers. "I'm not really sure."

Ms. Tremayne took a deep breath. "Dave?"

Dave leaned back in his desk, scratched his head, and

announced, "I think it would make 'em all take out more life insurance." The whole class broke up.

"I think it would make them free to be who they really are," I said suddenly, amazing myself. I never said anything in class. I *must* be tired to start shooting my mouth off.

"Brown-noser Bonnie!" hissed Mitch who happened to be sitting right behind me today. Mitch and I hadn't exactly hit it off from the start. Maybe it was because he reminded me too much of me a few years back. I swung around to face him but Ms. Tremayne's voice cut me off.

"Settle down, Steve. Turn around." I did, reluctantly.

"Now, Mitch, since you seem to have an opinion to express about this novel, why don't you share it with all of us?"

Mitch grinned insolently. "Sure, I got an opinion. I think it's all crap. This is what I think you should do with your stinkin' novel." He picked up his battered paperback and threw it in an expert arc into the garbage can.

There was a resounding thud as it landed in the metal can and then an ominous silence in the room. Ms. Tremayne turned kind of white and I figured she was about to explode. "All right, Mitch," she said in a voice so controlled I thought it might shatter, "go pick up that book and take it with you down to the office. You can use it to explain to Mr. Waters why you are no longer in this class."

I'd never seen this class pay attention like they were at that moment. A couple of kids who had been resting comfortably with their heads on their desk jumped when the book hit the can and were now so alert I thought they might start taking notes. Angeline, the blonde with the hair, stopped right in the middle of filing her nails and sat with her file poised like a dagger in mid-air. Mitch didn't miss the fact he had center stage and I guess he decided to go for broke because what he said to Ms. Tremayne then beat even my record for mouthing off at teachers. It was something I didn't recall having ever said to any woman.

The class gave kind of gasp — and then a second gasp — because, before I even stopped to think I'd swung around and decked Mitch Williams.

He sort of slid out the bottom of his desk and sat slumped on the floor with a slightly more stunned expression on his face than usual. Chaos broke out in class. Three or four people cheered. Sandra Wickman, Mitch's brainless girlfriend, started to bawl. "Mitch, are you all right?" she sniffled, kneeling beside him.

"Hope not," came the small, clear voice of little Robbie Hartly who Mitch made it a point to push around at least once a day.

I just sat there massaging my aching knuckles. Mitch had a real bony chin.

Then, just like a lion tamer, Ms. Tremayne took charge of the circus. "Sit down and stop blubbering," she told Sandra in a voice like a whip. "The rest of you, settle down. This is an English class, not World Federation of Wrestling. Take your novels and read chapter six. Do not speak. Do not move. Do not breathe. Read. *Now!*" There was instant silence and thirty-some heads bowed silently over their books. I noticed that Sandra had hers upside down but she was reading and turning pages as fast as she could go.

Then, Ms. Tremayne's blazing eyes settled on me. "Go to the office," she ordered. "And stay there until I have a chance to talk to you." I shrugged and got up. So much for her appreciating my once-in-a-lifetime effort at gallantry. But, it didn't really matter. Deep down, I'd known all along I'd never last the semester. And, right now, I was just too tired to care. I started for the door but, before I got there, it burst open. In charged Mr. Waters looking so hot and bothered that the five hairs on top of his head were waving in the breeze he created. "What's going on in here, Ms. Tremayne? Mr. Swifton next door just intercommed the office and said there was a riot going on in your class."

Ms. Tremayne looked mad enough to spit nails. When she caught up with Mr. Swifton he was going to be history. "There is *not* a riot going on here," she said. "As you can see we are silently reading our novels." Mr. Water's eyes swept the room and came to rest on Mitch, who was definitely *not* reading his novel. He was moaning and rubbing his chin.

"What happened to him?" demanded Waters.

Before Ms. Tremayne could open her mouth Sandra blurted out, "Steve slugged him!"

"He *what*?" Waters didn't wait for an answer from her. He just turned on me. But, before he could even get started yelling, the end-of-class bell rang. Nobody needed to be told twice to get out of there. In ten seconds flat the room was empty — except for Waters, Ms. Tremayne, me and Mitch, who was still listening to the little birdies sing in his head.

The door closed behind the last escaping student and Waters started in on me. "Well, Mr. Bonney, I guess this is about what I might have expected. We give you punks a second chance at school but all you're here for is to cause trouble. You think school is some back alley where you can exercise your street-gang mentality and intimidate people with your fists and you never have the faintest intention of doing a lick of work. But I won't put up with it. Get out of my school and don't come back."

I looked him in the eye. "You couldn't pay me enough to make me come back here." I spun around to leave and almost fell over Ms. Tremayne, who had stepped between me and the door.

"Hold it right there, Steve." She sounded real angry, and it took me a minute to realize that this time the anger wasn't directed at me. "There are a few things you ought to know, Mr. Waters. Number one is that Steve, here, happens to be one of about four students in this entire class who actually *do* some work and show some interest in learning something. If you had got around to checking my assignment book you'd have seen proof of that. Second, I think you should know the whole story of what happened here today." She strode over to where Mitch was now staring bleary-eyed at the ceiling. She gave Mitch a nudge with her toe. "Mitch, why don't you tell Mr. Waters what you said to me just before Steve punched you?"

Mitch's eyes widened and he came a notch closer to full consciousness. "No way!" he blurted out.

"Why not, Mitch?"

" 'Cause he'd kill me!"

Ms. Tremayne looked at Mr. Waters. Mr. Waters looked at Mitch. "Get up, Mitch," Mr. Waters growled. "You and I will continue this conversation in my office."

Mitch moaned. "I don't feel good."

"You may very likely feel worse soon," Mr. Waters said as he dragged Mitch to his feet. "Get going." Mitch stumbled toward the door throwing glances back over his shoulder like a nervous horse. Mr. Waters turned to follow him, then stopped and turned to me. "Under the circumstances, Mr. Bonney, I'll overlook your highly unsuitable behavior this time but, remember this, from now on you'd better walk softly in my school — "

" 'Cause you'll be watching me," I finished for him.

He gave me a cold look and walked out of the room.

That left me and Ms. Tremayne. We looked at each other and the silence got long and awkward. Finally

I cleared my throat. "Uh, thanks."

"What for?" she snapped impatiently. "I only told the truth."

I shrugged. "Yeah, well, uh, thanks anyway." I picked up my books and started to leave. Ms. Tremayne stopped me.

"Steve?"

I looked back.

"If you ever pull anything like that again I swear I'll throw you to the wolves. I don't need you to fight my battles for me."

"Yeah? And what were you gonna do about Mitch?"

Ms. Tremayne's eyes glittered. "Probably the same thing you did," she said. And I believed her.

Eighteen

As if the morning hadn't gone bad enough, Monday was the day we got an extra period of English in the afternoon. Mitch didn't show up and the word was out he was suspended until he brought his parents in to see Mr. Waters. The rest of the class was pretty quiet and I was keeping a low profile. So low, in fact, that I finally laid my head on my desk and gave in to a whole weekend of lost sleep.

The next thing I knew a hand was shaking me none too gently. I jumped, sat up straight, and looked around. The classroom was empty, except for Ms. Tremayne. She was standing there looking down on me with a scornful smile on her face. "Of all the people who've fallen asleep in my stimulating classes you're the first to stay asleep through the dismissal bell. You must have had quite a weekend."

"Yeah," I said, wearily, "I did."

She shook her head disgustedly. "It always amazes me how people who can find enough energy to tear around the country drinking beer all weekend can't seem to find enough energy to stay awake in school on Monday."

I sat up a little straighter and looked her right in the eye. "I wasn't drinkin' beer," I said, wondering why I cared what she thought I'd been doing. "If you really want to know I've spent the last forty-eight hours draggin' half-froze calves out of snowbanks and holdin' a cow's guts in while the vet did a Cesarean." There, that should turn her educated stomach, I thought with some satisfaction. Wrong again. All of a sudden Ms. Tremayne was looking at me with something close to respect.

"You're working on a ranch?"

I nodded. "Yeah. The Double C. It's way out in the hills about twenty miles away."

Ms. Tremayne's eyes lit up. "The Double C? Carl and Connie Johanneson?"

"Yeah. Why? You know 'em?" What would Carl and Connie be doing mixed up with my English teacher?

"Sure I know them! I worked for them the summer after grade nine. It was the best summer of my life. All I did was ride all day long. Broke four horses that summer."

Suddenly something Connie had said a long time ago clicked. Something about a girl breaking horses. "You didn't break a black mare named Ladysox, did you?"

"Ladysox! I not only broke her, I named her. What a great horse! She was my favorite of the whole bunch."

"That doesn't surprise me," I said, but Ms. Tremayne totally missed the sarcasm and just kept on smiling like I'd just made her day. And suddenly I realized that this was the first time I'd every really seen her smile. It made her look twenty times prettier and nowhere near as mad at the world.

"How are Connie and Carl? They were so good to me. I've been meaning to go back and see them ever since I came here to teach this winter, but there just hasn't been time."

I was having trouble keeping up with her train of thought. I didn't figure she could be *that* busy.

"You'd find time if you really wanted to," I said. She shot me a kind of startled look and I wondered if she was about to go back into her mad mode. But maybe I'd got just tired enough to be about half-crazy because all of a sudden I decided I might as well go for broke.

"I'll take you out with me right now. If you've got some clothes you can get dirty you can help with afternoon chores and I'll bring you back after supper."

"Steve, I can't."

"Would you rather grade English papers?"

Ms. Tremayne's flashed. "After the day I've had, I'd rather die than so much as *look* at an English paper."

"Okay, let's go."

We were halfway across the parking lot when I realized what I had done. I had just invited a girl — no, make that a lady — to ride with me in *Jesse's* truck. "Oh, uh, I forgot," I stammered. "My, uh, car is in the garage. It won't be ready for a couple of hours. Could we, uh, maybe take your car?" I could feel my face getting warm and I couldn't remember when I last felt this young and stupid.

Ms. Tremayne laughed. "Sure. My place is across the street." When we got there she handed me her keys. "Warm it up, will you while I run up and change my clothes."

Five minutes later she was back, out of breath and dressed in jeans and a torn old ski jacket. She slid behind the wheel. "So, how do you like my Camaro?"

I grinned. How did I like it? Just sitting in it made me want to get behind the wheel of a really hot car again so bad I was almost hoping she'd fall and sprain her wrist coming down the steps so I'd have to drive. But I wasn't about to give her the satisfaction of knowing how much I liked her car. I shrugged. "It's okay, I guess. We got a cow named after it out at the ranch." Ms. Tremayne gave me a strange look and laid a little rubber getting out of the parking lot. Fortunately the snowplows had been out and the roads were cleared off. I'd have hated to see that Camaro on ice the way Ms. Tremayne drove. The woman was a maniac. I didn't have any problem with fast driving; it was just that I would have liked it to be *me* doing the driving. I sucked in a quick breath as we screeched around one curve and I saw her smile. "Something wrong, Steve?"

I shook my head, "Nope, I was just thinkin' that for a sports car she don't have a whole lot of guts, does she?"

"Really?" said Ms. Tremayne. The next curve was even more interesting.

When we pulled into the ranch yard I noticed Carl and Jesse still weren't back. Connie flung open the barn door. I wished I could have taken a picture of her face when she saw an electric-blue Camaro skidding to a stop in front of the house and a strange woman getting out. I think she figured it was the Avon lady or something because she came striding up looking as mad as a wet cat. "Whatever it is you're selling . . ." she began but then Ms. Tremayne was running to meet her.

"Connie! It's so good to see you again," she said as she flung her arms around Connie.

"Lynne!" Connie hugged her, too, and then stepped back to get a good look at her. "Lynne Tremayne, where on earth did you come from?"

Ms. Tremayne laughed. "From school, Connie. I'm Steve's teacher."

I was out of the car by then, and Connie glanced from Ms. Tremayne to me and back again and just shook her head. But then she was all business again. "Well I'm sure going to want to hear more about you later, Lynne, but right now, Steve, you better dump those books in the house and put on some dirty clothes. I've got a rank old cow in the barn with a dim-witted calf that can't stand up without a boost and not a clue why God put those handy faucets on its mother. I've been trying to get him sucking for an hour now. The cow's chased me up the fence twice, kicked me once, and I've about had enough. Your turn to give it a shot."

I didn't suppose this was the usual way to entertain your English teacher when you brought her home for supper but she didn't seem too upset. All three of us trailed out to the barn.

The look in the cow's eyes told me I'd like her a whole lot better if she was tied up, so I dropped a lariat over her horns — she had a nice, sharp set — looped it around a post and handed the end to Connie so she could take up the slack if the cow moved. Then I climbed into the stall with her.

Tying her head had been a great idea. Her front end didn't cause me any trouble. But the minute I came near her she swiveled the rest of her body around and almost squashed me against the stall gate. I jumped out of the way and was standing there wondering what to do next when Ms. Tremayne suddenly appeared with another lariat in her hand. She reached through the rails of the gate and expertly flicked out a loop right behind the cow's hind feet. "Try giving her a little slack, Connie," she said. Connie loosened her rope a little and the cow automatically stepped back. Ms. Tremayne jerked the rope up taut, catching the cow's hind legs. Before the critter could fight back Ms. Tremayne tied the rope around a rail. *Then* the cow started to fight. But, tied tight at both ends like that there wasn't much she could do except raise a lot of dust.

I got the calf on its feet and pushed it gently in the direction of the cow's full bag. It wobbled and almost fell down. I caught it, steadied it, and gave it another gentle push in the right direction. The calf staggered forward, bumped its nose into the cow's side and stood there staring into space, its nose about two inches from a protruding, milk-filled teat. I sighed. This kid was not a fast learner.

I turned his head in the right direction, stuck my finger in his slimy mouth and guided the teat in with it. The calf backed up so fast he sat down in a heap. That spooked the cow and she went into another fit of thrashing around fighting the ropes and trying to kill me. I began to think longingly of veal cutlets. I stood the calf up and pointed him in the right direction again but as soon as I tried to shove the teat into his mouth he started backing up again.

Then Ms. Tremayne slipped in through the gate and stepped behind the calf. "You handle the front end. I'll push from behind."

It worked. I lined the calf's head up into position and stuffed in the teat. The bone-headed brat rolled his eyes and got his I'm-gettin'-out-of-here expression again but this time Ms. Tremayne was right behind him. There was nowhere to go.

Seconds passed. The calf just stood there with the teat in his mouth, looking mad. Then, his reflexes finally kicked in. His lips moved a little, his throat muscles flexed, then he made a little slurping sound. He swallowed. He went through all the motions again. And again and again, faster and stronger each time. His tail began to switch like it was providing power to run a pump. The sucking noises got louder and louder.

Ms. Tremayne and I stepped back. The calf never even noticed. He was taking in warm milk like he'd died and gone to calf heaven. The cow began to relax. Gradually, Connie gave her slack on the rope that held her head. She turned her head and gave the calf an affectionate lick across the back. He didn't even notice. He was too busy pumping. The Double C had one more cow calf act in business.

Ms. Tremayne and I looked at each other and grinned. "Nice job, Ms. Tremayne," I said.

She grinned. "Once someone has been my partner in a wrestling match with a cow, I generally give up a few formalities. My name's Lynne, Steve."

We were just untying the cow when Carl and Jesse showed up. It turned out Jesse had been working at the ranch the summer Lynne had been here so I soon found myself odd man out at a big reunion. Finally, we all headed for the house and while Lynne and Connie and me got cleaned up Jesse and Carl rustled us up some supper.

While we ate I found out some things that explained how Lynne Tremayne could walk out of her classroom, change into her jeans, and magically turn into a cowgirl. She'd been born a cowgirl. She grew up on a ranch on the other side of town and until she was fourteen she was her dad's right-hand man. Then, he was killed in an accident and her mother sold the ranch and moved to town. As usual, Carl and Connie had seen the chance to give a messed-up kid a break and brought her out to spend the summer doing the kind of work she loved. But the next year her mother had got a job in Calgary and Lynne hadn't been back to the Double C. Until now.

Everybody was laughing and telling blizzard stories and cattle stories and horse stories — I thought Lynne was going to fall off her chair laughing when she heard about me and Ladysox. Then, Connie asked Lynne how she liked being a teacher — and Lynne quit laughing. She even quit smiling. "It's not quite what I expected," she said, and changed the subject.

Nineteen

About nine o'clock Lynne said she had to go home and I got up to go back with her for Jesse's truck. Jesse started to ask where it was, once, but stopped when I shot him a look that threatened instant death. He grinned and gave me such an undisguised wink I didn't see how Lynne could miss it. I'd break his neck later.

We drove through the cold, clear, starlit night in silence for a while. Finally, I said, "So what did you mean when you said teaching wasn't what you expected?"

Lynne shot me a look. "After today do you really have to ask?"

I grinned. "Hey, you handled today okay. The way it looked to me, you won every round."

"Yeah, right up to the point where you finished things off with a knock out." She laughed bitterly.

"You're really bugged about that, ain't you?"

She tossed her hair back. "I'm bugged about a lot more than that." To my amazement her voice sounded like she was going to cry. "I was going to be such a great teacher, make kids think and care and really learn things.

I was never going to make all the mistakes I saw my own teachers making." She swallowed. "Oh, yeah, I was going to be different, all right."

"I think you *are* different." She flashed me a fiery look that showed her spirit wasn't completely broke. "Good different," I added quickly. "You don't just make us write down stuff, memorize it, and write it back down on the exams like Mr. Melnychuk does. You make us think."

"Yeah? Well maybe that's my first mistake. In case you hadn't noticed, nobody in that class — except maybe you — *wants* to think. They'd be a lot happier if I *did* just tell them what to memorize so they could pass the test."

"So, are you there to make 'em happy or to make 'em learn?"

Lynne sighed. "I don't suppose this could occur to somebody with *your* disposition but fighting the whole class every minute, every day is hard work. I got hired at Christmas to replace another teacher who couldn't stand the job any longer. I knew what I was getting into but I was so sure I could handle it. And I had so many happy memories of when I was a kid growing up around here I was really excited about coming back to Rock Creek. January was pretty bad but I kept telling myself that second semester I'd have a fresh start with a brand-new class and everything would be okay." She sighed. "Well, we're over a month into second semester and look at the mess I've made. For two cents I'd ditch the whole thing and go to work feeding cows for somebody. They may kick your teeth in but at least they don't talk back."

She brushed a hand across her eyes and left a smear of wetness across her cheek. "Hey," I said gently, "Ms. — Lynne — don't cry."

"I am not crying," she said fiercely, giving a big sniff and tromping on the gas a little harder.

I shook my head. Life was pretty weird. Here we were,

rocketing through a cold Alberta night like two astronauts alone in the emptiness of space. She was the good, middle-class kid who'd made all the right moves, set goals, and got what she'd thought she wanted — and now she hated it. And the one person she could talk to about it was a two-bit hood so messed up he couldn't be sure who was gonna get him first, the law or the *real* bad guys. But, right then, I didn't care about me. All I wanted was for Lynne not to get hurt. I hadn't wanted to protect a girl that way since I'd first met Tracey. And the whole idea scared me to death.

I was still thinking about it when Lynne suddenly muttered something not very teacherish under her breath and started to slow down. I checked the mirror — and saw my worst nightmare coming true. There was a cop car right behind us, all lit up like a Christmas tree and about to pull us over. Okay, Steve, I thought, my brain working cool and clear while my guts turned to ice. What do you do now?

I silently cursed myself for being such a fool. Here I am thinking all these big, gallant thoughts about keeping Lynne from getting hurt by a bunch of punk kids who don't want to listen to their English lessons and I drag her into what could be *real* trouble just by being any-where near her.

The car slowed to a stop on the shoulder. It flashed through my mind that if I was going to run, this was my one chance to jump out and disappear into the darkness before the cops had time to react. But if I did that I'd have to keep running. Because once I pulled a trick like that there was no way I could go back to being good old Steve Bonney, cowhand, again. I knew that, back in the fall, if I'd seen a cop car closing in on me like this I would have run for sure. But that was then. This was now. Things were different now. Maybe *I* was different now. I was going to have to stay cool and bluff my way through this. After all, it probably wasn't me that this cop was after.

"Lynne?" I gave her an easy grin. "How fast were you goin'?"

"You don't want to know," she said through her teeth.

"Oh."

"And don't you dare laugh."

"Trust me, Lynne. I ain't laughin'," I said, dead serious.

The cop car wheeled in behind us, the flashers making red and blue patterns on Lynne's face as she turned to look at me. "My driver's license is in the glove compartment. I suppose he's going to want to see it," she said sourly.

I hope that's all he wants to see, I thought as I opened the catch and reached in to get the license. If he asked me any hard questions — like what my name was — life could get complicated.

The cop tapped on Lynne's window. He was big and husky and he looked real pleased with himself. Lynne opened the window. "Good evening, miss," the cop said pleasantly. Lynne muttered something that might have been, "Hello." I could see she wasn't being the world's best sport about this.

"Beautiful night, isn't it?" the cop said, still pleasant as all get-out.

Lynne didn't say anything. "The sort of night a person should just drive along peacefully and enjoy, don't you think?" he went on with an irritating grin.

"I *was* enjoying it just fine till you came along," Lynne said. I groaned silently. Keep this up and you're gonna make him mad and then he'll get all officious and want to know everything including what I ate for breakfast yesterday. That same thought must have occurred to her because she managed to smile just enough to make the cop think she was joking.

He chuckled. "You'd have been able to enjoy it longer if you hadn't been exceeding the speed limit by twenty kilometers an hour. May I see your driver's license, please?"

I handed it to her and she passed it over. The cop studied it, checked the registration on the Camaro and then shone his flashlight around the inside of the car. Finally the light came to rest right in my eyes. "Who's your friend, Lynne?" the cop asked like he'd known her all his life.

"Steve Bonney."

"And where have you and Steve been this evening?" Obviously, the guy must have a pretty boring life.

"Out to the Double C Ranch." Lynne was being real polite ever since he'd told her how much she'd been over the speed limit. Even an English teacher could do enough math to figure the size of ticket if this cop decided to go for broke.

"And where are you going now?"

"To Rock Creek."

"Do you live there?"

"I do. I'm taking Steve to pick up his truck,"

"And where is the truck?"

Lynne shot me an uneasy glance that I didn't totally understand and then said, "At the garage."

I cursed myself some more. Didn't I *have* to lie about enough things just to stay out of jail? Why did I have to lie to Lynne about the truck just to save my pride? Now if this nosy cop decided to spice up his night with an exciting look at my truck he'd find out I'd lied and get real curious about why. Someday, I was gonna quit living like this. Someday, I was gonna be able to look any cop in the eye and tell him anything he needed to know — including where to get off.

"Could I see some identification from you, please Steve?" the cop said.

I thought fast. I could say I left it at home. And what if this genius wanted to know why I was planning to take my truck home without my driver's license? I decided to gamble. "I left it in my truck," I said, meeting his eyes.

"I see." The cop looked thoughtful. "I'll be just a minute," he said, striding off toward his car. He still had Lynne's license and registration in his hand. Lynne watched him go and stuck her tongue out at his beefy back. I started to laugh. That was probably the only thing that kept me from having a nervous breakdown while I waited for him to come back.

Finally, he strolled back, stuck his head in the window, and handed back Lynne's papers. "Everything's fine," he said. "Just wanted to double-check the ownership on the car. You better be careful where you leave this thing parked, Lynne. Did you know Camaros are one of the top three favorites among car thieves?" He shone the light in my face again. "And your friend here fits the general description of a car thief the Calgary police have been on the watch for so it never hurts to check."

Lynne gave the officer a thousand-watt smile. "No, it doesn't. And thanks for the warning about the thieves. May I go now?"

The cop shook his head. "No, not yet, Lynne."

The smile lost a little wattage. "What's wrong, officer?"

Now *he* smiled. "I haven't written your ticket yet."

Ten minutes later we were pulling into Rock Creek and I remembered I'd better do some fast thinking about where my truck supposedly was. "I'll just walk from your place," I said and Lynne nodded and kept on driving. She hadn't been real talkative since old Chubby Cheeks had snagged her for a hundred and twenty bucks. But, instead of pulling up in front of her place, she went right on by, hung a left, and pulled into the school parking lot where Jesse's truck sat all alone like a decaying carcass in the middle of the prairie. She drove up beside the truck and stopped. "No point in walking when I can deliver you to the door," she said with a teasing grin.

I shook my head. "Okay, how did you know this was what I drove?"

She laughed. "I've been watching you drive into this parking lot every morning since you came here. You remind me of a dog trying to find a place to bury something when you look for a parking place to hide your truck."

"Hey. Let's get one thing straight. It's not mine. Jesse's just letting me borrow it."

Lynne took a hard look out the window. "It *is* Jesse's." She sounded surprised. "That's the same truck he was driving when I worked at the Double C seven years ago. I thought it was about a hundred years old *then*."

I got out of the car and then thought of a question. "So, if you knew all along my truck *wasn't* in the garage, why'd you go along with me?"

She grinned wickedly. "I was looking forward to seeing your face when I brought you back to it. Besides, maybe I wanted your company."

We said good night and I was more than relieved that Jesse's truck actually started. I drove home slowly, thinking — and making sure not to attract our friendly neighborhood cop. I felt real bad about Lynne's hundred and twenty bucks. But the incident with the cop hadn't been a total loss, I thought, smiling tiredly to myself. While I was putting her license away I'd managed to find out something I'd really wanted to know.

Lynne Tremayne had just turned twenty-two. That wasn't so old.

Twenty

*J*ust when it seemed like winter would never end, all of a sudden it was over. Overnight, the snow melted and the world started to turn green. It was then that I realized just how beautiful that country really was and that, somehow, I'd started thinking of it as home. I kept reminding myself it couldn't last. But I wasn't having much luck getting myself to listen. The past I'd left behind seemed further and further away. Sometimes it seemed like I'd imagined the whole thing, that my life here on the Double C was all that was real — until I'd catch a glimpse of the white scar on my arm. Romero didn't shoot imaginary bullets.

Ranch work slowed down from the numbing grind of cold-weather calving to mostly routine chores with an occasional crisis just to keep us from getting rusty. School was, well, school was school. I guess the most amazing thing about it was that I was still there at all. In a little over two months the semester would be over and it looked like I was actually going to stick it out. I just kept trudging off to school and memorizing my social studies and trying to shift gears fast enough to remember to do my own thinking in English class. We'd got to the part where we were doing a lot of writing, stories and poems and stuff, and I liked it. I used to write poems sometimes when I lived in Vancouver. It was a way to get out a lot of things you felt but could never really say to anybody. I got good marks on the poetry part — but Ms. Tremayne was still giving pretty lousy marks on my spelling and grammar but she was giving me some extra help with them and, slowly, I was catching on.

At school she was still Ms. Tremayne and we never exchanged a word that didn't have to do with English, but a girl named Lynne was spending all her spare time at the Double C. And one day I realized that the times when she *wasn't* around there was a whole lot of emptiness on the ranch.

I kept telling myself I was crazy to even think that way. To Lynne I was just a kid who was fun to hang around with and she'd laugh if I ever even asked her out. And I had no right to involve a nice girl in a life that was messed up as bad as mine. Not after what had happened to Tracey.

But, I might as well have been talking to the prairie wind, because one Saturday I went ahead and asked her anyway.

We were out riding and Lynne's hair was blowing in the wind and she was laughing and she sure didn't *look* like my English teacher should look. Maybe that's why I got up the nerve to say it. "Hey, uh, Lynne?"

"Yeah, Steve?" She looked back over her shoulder at me. She was *always* looking back at me because she always rode ahead. She rode the same way she drove and there weren't any helpful cops out here to keep her slowed down. I nudged Buster, my bay gelding, to catch up to Ladysox, who'd been shamelessly stolen right from under me.

"You wanna go to a movie or something in Calgary tonight?"

There was a long silence and I started feeling like a fool. "I'm older than you think I am."

"You mean you didn't turn nineteen last July 17?"

I stared at her. "How'd you find that out?"

She smiled. "I checked your school registration form."

"Why?"

She shrugged. "I was curious about you."

"So, how does nineteen on July 17 compare with twenty-two on February 20?"

Lynne's eyes widened. "How did you know my age?"

It was my turn to smile. "Checked your driver's license."

Lynne reined Lady in on top of a windy hill. "You've got a lot of nerve." Her eyes were flashing.

I met her look. "So have you."

We sat there and watched the wind-blown clouds race by for a minute. "Okay," Lynne said.

"Okay, what?"

"Okay, Steve Bonney, you've got a date."

I grinned. But I wished she hadn't said it in a way that reminded me I wasn't even a real person.

We rode slowly back, side by side. We were nearly home when I asked, "So it doesn't bother you that I'm a couple of years younger?"

Lynne gave me a long, searching look and slowly shook her head, "You're not younger, Steve. You were just born later."

I thought about that for a long time — and I finally decided she was right.

"So, what movie do you want to see?" I asked, bracing myself to be polite when she picked one of those mushy movies where all the characters ever do is talk and bawl and then talk and bawl some more.

Lynne shrugged. "You're paying, you get to pick. I don't care." She paused and then grinned. "As long as it's got lots of fast cars and fist fights."

I had a feeling the lady and I were gonna get along just fine.

I wondered what it would be like to go out into the real world again after a winter holed up like a hibernating bear. I also wondered if I was out of my mind for daring to try it at all.

But it was dark when we hit the city and that made me feel a whole lot better. Shadowy streets, dark movie theatre. I was still invisible. And safe. The movie was stupid, but fun. Lynne and I sat there holding hands like a couple of junior high kids — old-fashioned junior high kids, that is. On the way home she asked if I wanted to drive. I just smiled and shook my head. "You go ahead, I'll let you know if you make any mistakes. Anyhow," I added before she had time to hit me, "you handle cops so much better than I do." She did hit me then.

Connie had invited Lynne to spend the weekend at the ranch so when we got back we just sat in the car talking for a long time. Then a coyote started howling up on the hill, the dog started barking, and somebody switched a light on. We figured it was time to go in — like good, old-fashioned junior high kids. There was a long, awkward pause while we sat staring at each other in the romantic beams of the yard light. Okay, I'd proved you could date your English teacher. But, could you *kiss* your English teacher? There was only one way to find out.

It was a sweet and gentle kiss, but when I closed my eyes it was Tracey's face I saw.

For the next couple of months I was about as close to happy as I could ever remember being. You really have to try hard to be miserable in the spring with everything green and warm and the hillsides covered with crocuses and calves and summer coming.

Besides, I was about half in love with Lynne, which maybe explains why I started writing poems again and running off at the mouth about crocuses and stuff. I had a great girlfriend, the best job of my life, the Johannesons treated me like family, and Jesse — well, I worried some about Jesse. He had worked so hard and so long to save the valley and the final hearing was getting close. I didn't want to see Jesse get hurt.

I'd stuck out the semester at school. The fact I hadn't quit was almost as important to me as passing the final exams. But they were pretty important. For the first time in my life I actually studied. I gave those exams my best shot but somewhere in the back of my mind that kid who'd been failing grade seven kept telling me it might not be good enough.

On the twenty-sixth of June, it was so hot in town that the asphalt was sticky when I got out of the truck in the school parking lot. I was sweating by the time I got to the office but I wasn't sure how much was from the temperature and how much was from tension. I was just as nervous as I'd been the first time I walked in here on that cold day in February. Then, I was sure I wouldn't make it at school. Today I was going to find out if I'd been right.

The report cards were all laid out on the counter in alphabetical order ready to be picked up. I started digging through the pile. Foster, Frannelli, Fyten, Glenn, Granville . . . What? It wasn't here. I tried again. Went all the way back to the E's and worked my way up through the F's and right to the end of the G's. Garrett just wasn't there anywhere.

"Hi, Steve," Lynne's voice brought me out of my daze. "The moment of truth, huh?"

"Yeah, but my report card's not here."

"What? Sure it is. I put it there myself half an hour ago. Here, let's see."

She took the stack out of my hand, started riffling through from the top, and came out with the fifth one. "What do you call that, Steve Bonney?" she teased.

Lynne looked at me standing there like an idiot willing myself not to turn red and laughed and shook her head. "You really *are* nervous, aren't you?"

I shrugged. "Sort of," I said casually.

"Well, go ahead, open it."

I did. There were two slips of paper in the envelope. The top was social studies. The mark was seventy. I grinned. I still didn't understand what most of that stuff had really been about but, man, could I memorize.

I looked up at Lynne who was shamelessly reading over my shoulder. "Not bad," she said, as if she hadn't already checked it out a long time ago. "Well, don't you want to know what you got in English?"

I took a deep breath. "I dunno," I said, remembering that final exam. I figured I must have blown it pretty bad. I was there over half an hour longer than anyone else just trying to get the thing finished. Slowly, I pulled out the second sheet. It was a moment I wasn't sure I wanted to share with my English teacher or my girlfriend.

I looked at the mark. Eighty-five. What? Maybe that first number was a three not an eight. I held it up to the light. It was an eight.

"Need glasses, Steve?" Lynne asked, grinning.

I stared at her accusingly. "You cheated for me."

Lynne's eyes flashed angrily. "I *what?* You better get one thing straight right now, Steve. I don't cheat for *any-body*. Not even you. Least of all you. And just to make sure I didn't after I marked your paper I took it to a friend of mine who teaches English in High River. *He* gave you eighty-seven. Trust me, Steve. Every mark you got, you earned." She paused. "You know, Steve, all that's wrong with you is that you refuse to believe in yourself."

Well, it wasn't *all* that was wrong with me. But she could be partly right. It's hard to believe in somebody who isn't real.

Suddenly Lynne glanced at her watch. "Come on." She picked up her jacket. "That report card needs celebrating. I'll buy you a milkshake down at the drive-in."

I gave her an unbelieving look. "Here? In Rock Creek?" Ever since we'd been going out there'd always been one unwritten rule between us. Around town she was never anything to me but my English teacher.

Lynne grinned wickedly. "The school term ended four minutes ago. For the next two months I'm a human being, not a teacher. And you just quit being a student. So let's get outa this dump!" She grabbed my hand and practically dragged me out the door.

On the way out we almost ran into my old buddy Mitch, coming to get his report card. If I was him I wouldn't have bothered. He'd managed to get himself let back into school after our little set-to in English but I doubted he'd handed in a single assignment in the last three months. I thought his bloodshot eyes were going to pop out of his head when he saw Lynne and me holding hands and from the smell of him he must have already celebrated year-end by drowning a barrel or two of beer. The beer must have made him even more mouthy than usual because he muttered a comment about the two of us that even beat his own record for being crude.

I started to turn around but Lynne's grip on my hand tightened. "Forget it, Steve!" she said in a fierce whisper. "He isn't worth the trouble."

I wasn't so sure about that but this time I gave in and we walked out into the blazing sunshine and out of sight of Mitch — forever, I hoped.

Twenty-one

We got the milkshakes — in the Camaro, of course — and cruised around drinking them, enjoying the air-conditioning and listening to the stereo. Lynne had one serious flaw in her character — she liked country music. But, she was wearing me down. I was *almost* beginning to like *Cadillac Ranch* ten times a trip — which was how often she played it. Almost.

We drove through the park along the river. With the first really hot weather of the summer the snow was melting in the mountains and the water was high and fast. A bunch of cars and people up along the highway bridge caught my attention. "Hey, what's goin' on up there?"

"That?" Lynne said, her voice scornful. "That's just the local heroes out trying to kill themselves again."

"What?"

"You never stick around town long enough after school to see it," she said, pulling the car into a parking spot on the breakwater and turning off the engine. "They've been at it ever since the hot weather hit and the river came up. Jumping off the top of the bridge into the river. Isn't that the dumbest, most dangerous stunt you've ever seen?"

I grinned. "Not quite. In Vancouver we used to ride the ferries out to the edge of the harbor, jump off and race each other back to shore. We had a diving place, too. Up the coast where there was a cliff about forty feet high above the ocean. Worked fine as long as the tide was in."

Lynne shook her head. "How'd you ever manage to live to grow up?"

"Am I grown up?" I asked, laughing to drive away the cold shiver that ran through me as I remembered a kid who *hadn't* lived to grow up. He broke his neck when he miscalculated a dive. But he'd been drinking that day. However much time I spent drunk or stoned in those days, I only dived cold sober.

We got out of the car and stood leaning against the fender, taking in the show. There were about a dozen kids diving, mostly boys but a couple of girls, too. It was dangerous enough but not as dangerous as it had looked from a distance. They weren't diving into the main channel of the run-off swollen river. There was a backwater at the south edge of the bridge, a deep, calm pool mostly cut off from the main channel by a gravel bar. It was the pool they were diving into.

I watched as a little, dark-haired grade ten kid balanced easily on the railing for a couple of seconds and then jumped, feet-first. There was a hugh splash and a loud cheer from the crowd as he hit the water. I remembered the rush of adrenalin, the feel of an eagle plummeting through thin air, and the jolt of icy water. A wave of envy swept through me as he surfaced, laughing, and swam to shore.

One of the girls dived next. And I mean *dived*, not jumped. It looked good enough for the Olympics, a perfect arc of sleek white bathing suit and long, tanned legs against the cloudless blue sky. I gave her a low, appreciative whistle — and Lynne gave me a sharp elbow in the ribs. The girl hit the water clean as an arrow, hardly even making a splash. A woman with an expensive-looking camera shot a picture of the dive and another of the girl climbing, smiling, out of the water. Probably her mother, I thought — and then changed my mind. If her mother caught her doing anything that dangerous she'd be dragging her out of there by the ear, never mind the picture. I glanced up at the railing again and froze.

There, teetering dangerously, red hair flaming in the sun and baggy, fluorescent-pink flowered shorts flapping in the breeze, was Mitch. As usual, he was mouthing off to somebody. I couldn't hear the words but I could see him looking back over his shoulder, talking to somebody. I felt Lynne go tense beside me.

"Mitch!" she almost whispered. "He's too drunk to stand up, let alone . . ."

Right then his foot slipped. He tumbled off the railing in an out-of-control somersault, grazed a support pillar with one shoulder, and just kept falling like a bird shot out of the sky. The crowd gave one shocked gasp and then froze into horrified silence as Mitch narrowly missed the gravel bar and splashed heavily into the water — the white-capped water of the main channel.

The scene was like a freeze frame from a movie. No one spoke. No one moved. Only the river. It just kept rushing by like nothing had happened. Suddenly, my brain unfroze and I realized that, of the whole crowd, we were the only ones downstream from where Mitch went in. If he had one chance — which I doubted — I was it. The next thing I knew I was tearing off my shirt and sneakers.

"No, Steve!" Lynne screamed, but I was already running along the bank, looking for Mitch in the foaming brown water. I couldn't see anything in there. And then

— a flash of fluorescent pink! Mitch's awful taste in clothes might just save his miserable life yet. I sucked in a deep breath and dived, aiming downstream of where I'd seen the flash of pink.

I'd been right. The cold of that snowmelt water *was* a jolt. So much of a jolt that it knocked the wind right out of me. I fought for air and felt the current taking control of me. How did I expect to drag Mitch out of here if I couldn't even drag myself out? Just then I saw the flash of pink again coming up even with me, a little farther over in the middle of the channel. I swam for all I was worth, remembering riptides and undertows and all the dirty tricks the ocean had ever thrown at me. It didn't have much this little two-bit mountain river didn't have. Blindly, I reached out — and my hand touched something. Hair! Mitch's long, curly hair. I tangled my fingers in it the way I used to do with my horse's mane when I was a kid riding bareback. I felt the current try to tear Mitch loose but I held on for all I was worth and began fighting my way across the channel toward the bank.

It wasn't easy. The power of that force sweeping me downstream was unbelievable and the cold of the water was beginning to wear me down. The current was pulling me out into midstream again and I couldn't fight it much longer. Mitch was a dead weight, like trying to drag a block of concrete behind me. I wasn't going to make it.

Suddenly, a raft of driftwood swept by and instinctively I reached out for it. I caught a branch and hung on. We were still racing downstream but at least it was a chance to rest and get my breath back. And right then Mitch got his breath back, too. Up to now, he'd been dead to the world — maybe just plain dead for all I knew — but all of a sudden he opened his eyes and started thrashing around, flailing at me with his fists, doing his best to wrap an arm around my throat and choke me.

There's only one thing you can do when somebody you're saving from drowning goes crazy like that. I did it. And I hate to admit how much I enjoyed it. I let him have it on the jaw with my fist and he subsided into a nice quiet block of concrete again.

Then I was hanging onto the raft of driftwood again. It swept around a bend and the power of the current swung it toward the bank. This was my chance. I swam for that bank with all the strength I had left. I got my head far enough above water once to get a look at the shore and caught a glimpse of what looked like the start of the Boston Marathon. Dozens of people were running along the bank, jumping over rocks and deadfall, all trying to catch up to me and Mitch. It was the funniest thing I'd seen in a long time. A wave slapped me in the face and I choked and forgot all about how funny this all was.

Then, I felt gravel under my feet and I was stumbling through shallow water and the river was full of people wanting to help and mainly getting in my way as I tried to get good old Mitch to stand on his own two feet and walk. He was coming to again, muttering and groaning and stumbling through the water. Finally, his eyes actually focused and he recognized me.

"Bonney!" he croaked. "You hit me again! You." He started cussing, calling me every name he could think of. The thought of throwing him back in did cross my mind but the whole thing was starting to strike me as pretty funny again. I started to laugh and finished dragging him up to the bank like some big, bone-headed fish I'd just landed. I was still laughing — and keeping a firm grip on a handful of his hair when out of nowhere the woman who'd been taking the diving pictures appeared, stuck her expensive camera in my face, and snapped a picture. For some reason I couldn't quite focus on, getting my picture taken annoyed the heck out of me and I might have told her so if I hadn't collapsed about then.

Hands dragged me up on the grass and I just lay there shivering for a few minutes, too tired and cold to move. People were flapping around bringing me blankets, trying to rub the circulation back into my hands and feet, and just generally getting on my nerves. Finally I sat up, shook off a few dozen helpful nurses and turned to Lynne who had her arm around me and was not about to be shaken off. "Let's get out of here," I croaked, not sounding one bit better than Mitch had. She helped me up and we headed for the car. A couple of Mitch's buddies were dragging him off to a car, too. He seemed in pretty good shape considering what he'd been through. I guess it's true what they say about drunks being able to relax when they take a fall.

Mitch never did say thank you. If he had I think it might have ruined my faith in human nature.

Twenty-two

Nobody was home at the Double C when I dripped my way into the bunkhouse — Jesse and I had moved back there for the summer — so I just had a shower, mopped up the puddles, and washed my clothes. I never got around to mentioning my unexpected little swim. Fortunately, Lynne had to go to Calgary for her grandma's birthday that weekend so she didn't get a chance to blab the whole story either. By Monday the whole thing was history, a finished chapter of my life that went along with school and town and good old Mitch, none of which I planned to see anything of for a good long time.

I was changing the oil in the farm truck Monday morning — that is I would have been if Jesse ever got back from town with the oil. At last I saw — and heard — his truck come rattling around the corner so I figured it was safe to go ahead and drain the old oil. I crawled under the four-by-four and unscrewed the plug, which was in there so tight I lost half the skin off my knuckles and all of my temper before I got it loose. I was still

under there, muttering, when I heard Jesse's truck pull up
and the door slam. The next thing I knew Jesse was prod-
ding me with his foot and saying something like, "Hey,
hero, come on out. I've got to see this 'movie star look'
for myself." I didn't have the faintest clue what he was
talking about and I was in no mood to find out.

"Don't hassle me, Firelight," I growled, sliding out
and bringing the pail of dirty oil with me, "or you'll find
out what oily hair is really all about."

Jesse's grin just got wider and more irritating. "Aw
come on, Steve. Give me a little flash of that 'devil-may-
care smile' of yours," he said, dissolving into laughter as
he read something from the front page of the *Rock Creek
Roundup.* I made a grab for the paper but he jerked it away.
"Oh, no you don't! Don't you go putting your greasy little fingerprints on my souvenir picture. If you wash up
real careful I might let you autograph it for me later."

I made another grab. "Let me see that, Firelight,
you . . ."

"Okay, okay, just get all that 'selfless, unthinking
bravery' under control there, city boy, and I'll let you read
it. Look, but don't touch, okay?" He spread the paper out
on the hood of the truck and there I was, face-to-face with
me. Me, soaking wet, wearing nothing but my jeans, a
grin, and a fair amount of mud, dragging good old Mitch
out of the river and looking happy as if I was in my right
mind about it all. Underneath the big, bold print read,
THE FACE OF COURAGE.

In spite of the hot sunshine I felt a cold chill. My picture, plastered all over the front page of the paper. Then I
went from scared to mad.

"What? Who wrote this crap?"

"Just settle down and listen, city boy, I'll read you
the story. Believe me, it gets better." He started reading
out loud:

What started out as high-spirited high school highjinks last Thursday nearly ended in tragedy for an ill-fated local teenager. Eighteen-year-old Mitch Williams was just one of many local teenagers taking part in the highly dangerous sport of diving from the highway bridge into a backwater of the high-running Elkhead River.

Unfortunately, his daring was greater than his balance, and just as he was prepared to leap into the water his foot slipped, sending him plummeting, not into the comparative safety of the quiet backwater but into the foaming floodwaters of the river's death-dealing main channel. Before the horror-stricken eyes of the watching crowd Mitch was instantly swept downstream to what seemed like certain death.

But then, out of nowhere, like a knight in shining armour, a young hero rose to save the day. With a selfless, unthinking bravery rarely seen these days nineteen-year-old Steve Bonney of the Double C Ranch, dived in to save his friend.

Friend? I laughed so loud at that one Jesse stopped and gave me a dirty look. Then he went on.

For several tense minutes it was a close contest between the river and the boy to see who would claim the prize . . .

I groaned. Give me a break. *Nobody's* got enough imagination to call Mitch Williams a prize.

But the resiliency of youth and clean living were obviously on Steve Bonney's side.

This time it was Jesse who stopped and rolled his eyes skyward before he could go on.

Moments later, exhausted but victorious, his handsome face lit by a devil-may-care smile, the blond-haired teenager with the movie-star look tenderly lifted his shaken companion into the waiting arms of the eager helpers on shore.

"Hey, Steve," Jesse interrupted himself, "what *were* you grinning at?"

"I was grinning because I'd just slugged Mitch Williams and I was considering doing it again," I growled.

Jesse raised an eyebrow and went on reading.

Though thoroughly chilled by the river's icy waters, both boys were able to walk away apparently undamaged by their ordeal.

Steve Bonney, hero, the town of Rock Creek salutes you.

Jesse folded the paper and put it carefully out of my reach. "Well," he asked cheerfully, "What does being a hero feel like?"

"I feel," I said slowly, through my teeth, "like I'm gonna throw up. *Who* wrote that, Jesse?"

"Oh it sounds like the fine hand of Violet Prentice. Dizzy-looking dame with gray hair and glasses. She's always hovering around town with her camera looking for 'human interest'" pictures."

"Yup," I said, remembering, "that'd be the one. But how come the paper actually *prints* this stuff? If anybody wrote anything that bad in English class Lynne would make 'em eat it."

"Paper belongs to a guy named Henry Prentice," Jesse said with a grin.

And that pretty well explained that.

I spent the next few days in a state of permanent embarrassment. Of course as soon as Connie and Carl saw the paper *they* had to replay the whole incident. And then Lynne came out a couple of days later and read the whole story out loud over coffee — and assigned old Violet an English grade of minus thirty-two percent.

That was all bad enough but when a guy I'd never seen before in my life came out to repair a tractor tire, took one look at me, and said, "Hi, Steve, how's it feel to be a local hero?" I'd had about enough. That was also when I started to get real worried. If this guy could recognize me from my picture so easily, who else could? And how did I manage to go from being practically invisible out here in the middle of nowhere to being on the front page of the paper? And why couldn't Violet What's-Her-Name have fallen in the river and saved all this trouble?

It was a hot July morning. I was tearing the rotten planks off the old bull pen and nailing on heavy, new spruce two by sixes. It was the kind of job that took a lot of muscle and not much brain. It should have been perfect for me. But, it gave me a chance to think about some things I managed to keep pushed to the back of my mind most of the time. Things like the fact that it was July already. The job at the Double C was supposed to last through calving time. That had been over months ago. Were Carl and Connie just too good-hearted to tell me it was time to go? And even if they really did have enough work for both me and Jesse, I still couldn't stay much longer. The past would catch up to me again, just like it did at Pop's place. And, when it did, there was no way I wanted good people like the Johannesons to be in the line of fire.

And then there was Lynne. I wiped the sweat off my face and just stood there, staring out across the pasture, thinking about her — and wondering how I could be crazy enough to think it could work out for us. Just then, as if my thoughts had been a magnet, a bright blue dot came sizzling down the road. The dot turned into a Camaro and the Camaro turned into the lane. I grinned. When Lynne was here I never had any trouble believing the two of us were meant to be together.

The Camaro screeched to a stop in front of the barn and Lynne jumped out and came running over to the corral. "I saw you leaning on the fence, staring down the road when you were supposed to be working," she teased. "Wait'll I tell Connie.

I just grinned. "Maybe there was somethin' worth starin' at."

"Flattery will get you nowhere."

"What do you mean, flattery? I wasn't talkin' about you. I was lookin' at that new colt out there in the pasture," I said, straight-faced.

Lynne hauled off and walloped me one on the arm. "Shut up and build your fence, hot shot," she said, bending over to pick up the other end of the plank I was working on. As she did, an envelope fell out of her pocket. She picked it up. "Oh, yeah, I almost forgot. I stopped at the corner and picked up the Double C mail. There's a letter for you." She handed me the envelope.

I stared at her, unbelieving. "What?"

She laughed. "Don't get much mail, do you?"

That was the understatement of the year. I didn't get any mail. You're not *supposed* to get mail when nobody's supposed to know where you are. I turned the letter over and studied the postmark. Fenton, Alberta. Pop and Beau. *Where* the letter came from didn't bother me near as much as how it happened to find me. I read the envelope:

Steve Bonney (at least they hadn't gone and sent it to Steve Garrett!)

Double C Ranch

Rock Creek, Alberta

It was Beau's writing. But how could he know where I was? The last anybody in Fenton had heard from me was that phone call to Raine from Cochrane nine months ago. And then *I* hadn't even known I was going to be here. And if I'd somehow left a trail my brother could follow, who else might be following it, too?

"Steve?" Lynne's face had gone serious. "What's wrong? Aren't you going to open it?"

I forced a grin and jammed the letter into my pocket. "Naw, it can wait. Hurry up and get your end of that plank in place, we're wastin' the boss's time."

I'd never built a fence so fast in my life. Half an hour later with Lynne muttering and complaining about slivers and slave drivers we headed for the house for coffee. I locked myself in the bathroom and ripped open the letter. As I pulled it out of the envelope what looked like a newspaper clipping fell out and almost landed in the toilet. I picked it up. It was the picture of me dragging Mitch out of the river.

But, how did Beau get hold of a *Rock Creek Roundup*? Then I noticed the printing at the top of the page. The *Calgary Journal*. The *Calgary Journal!* What? How? I checked the small print under the picture. Courtesy of *Rock Creek Roundup*. The *Journal* had somehow got hold of the story — considerably toned down from Violet's version — and the photo and reprinted it and — a lump of ice settled in my stomach — spread my picture *and* my address all over southern Alberta.

I unfolded the letter.

Dear Steve *Bonney*, (You've got to be kiddin'!)

If I hadn't known it was you from your face and the bullet scars on your arm the name would have been a dead giveaway.

All this time we've been thinking you must be back out west or in the States or dead in an alley somewhere and you turn up less than four hours away. You could've at least called to let us know you were okay. But I guess from the new name and all you're still into big-time cops and robbers and you figure you've buried yourself good and deep out there. Well, as you can see from the clipping, that's not exactly true anymore. Geez, Steve you know less about being inconspicuous than anybody I know. You don't go rescuing somebody in front of the whole town when you're hiding out! But I guess *you* do.

Anyhow, what I had to tell you was that your old friend Russ Donovan's back in town. He ended up with just a suspended sentence for that whole mess at the Quarter Circle last fall. He was waving a copy of this article around in the bar the other night and bragging about how he was going to settle a score with you real soon now he knew where to find you. But that wasn't the worst part. He also said Romero was going to be out of jail next week and would be real interested in seeing you again, too.

I wish you'd just turn yourself in to the law before those two end up blowing you away some dark night. But I know you won't do it so I figured you should at least be ready for them.

Pop and me are fine. J.C. Kincaide finally got over his heart attack, lost thirty pounds, and is half reasonable to work for now — sometimes. Raine sends her love — I wouldn't have put that in but I know she's going to make me show her the letter before I mail it. She also wants me to tell you she's started training Rebel Yell for barrel racing. He's doing pretty good — if you don't count the time he took the bit in his teeth and ran half a mile before she got him turned around.

Gotta go. Oh, by the way, I passed all my grade eleven subjects — including biology. My worst mark was 65. In English, naturally. Sure was glad you left all your poems behind or it might have been a lot worse.

Keep in touch. If you can't write a letter just keep on leaping tall buildings with a single bound and getting your picture in the paper.

Beau

P.S. Be careful, Steve.

I read the letter through about three times and then just stood there staring at the paper, laughing to myself. Tears stung behind my eyes. Good old honest Beau. He still couldn't decide if he loved me or hated me. All of a sudden I missed him so bad that for two cents I would've jumped in my car — make that Jesse's truck — and headed for Fenton.

There was a loud knock on the bathroom door. "Steve? You die in there or what?" Lynne asked impatiently.

"Don't get your shirt in a knot. I'm just finishin' an article in National Geographic about a chimp that can speak English."

"Really? He'd have probably got the highest mark in my English 23 class."

Twenty-three

*J*esse and I had the afternoon off and Lynne talked
us both into riding to the Wolfsong Valley with her.
She had never seen it and after hearing everybody
talk about it so much her curiosity was killing her. And
she figured Jesse was worrying so much about the final
hearing coming up this week that he needed something
to distract him. I didn't argue about going. It would be my
last chance to see the valley again before I hit the road.

When we topped the ridge and Lynne got her first look
at the valley her reaction was pretty much the same as
mine had been. For a long time she just sat there and
stared. Finally, she turned to Jesse. "Fight for it, Jesse.
Don't ever let them have it." Then, before Jesse could
answer, she turned back for another look at it. "Jesse,
what's that?" She was pointing to a thin brown scar in
the deep green of the spruce forest.

Jesse stared at it and his eyes narrowed. "I don't
know," he said slowly, "but I'm about to find out." He
touched Firebird with his spurs and the roan headed down
the steep trail in a cloud of dust. Lynne and I followed.

The brown scar was a road. Fresh as a still-bleeding cut, it came in from the forestry road to the west and slashed arrow-straight through the trees, finally widening out into a campsite by the river. Two big bulldozers were still sitting there.

Jesse pulled Firebird to a stop in the clearing. "The buzzards," he said bitterly. "The Valley isn't even dead yet but they're circling the body."

"That's not legal, is it Jesse?" Lynne asked angrily. "They can't start clearing before the final decision is in."

Jesse took a deep breath. "Yeah, technically they can. They'll call this an 'exploratory base of operations' or something. They're so bloody sure they're going to win this thing," he added, his eyes smouldering with anger.

I looked over at the bulldozers. "Hang on to my horse a minute, Lynne," I said, getting off and handing her the reins. I walked over to the nearest dozer. There was a toolbox on the back, and in it a pair of pliers. This would be simple. I started tracing the fuel line, looking for an inconspicuous spot. There. There was a place in the shade of a blade mount and . . .

A hard hand gripped my shoulder. I turned and came face-to-face with Jesse. "What do you think you're doing?" he growled.

I grinned. "Just givin' these guys somethin' to keep them occupied. One crimp in the fuel line and they'll spend the next week tryin' to figure out why this thing won't run right."

Jesse shook his head. "Uh-uh. We're fighting this war clean. So far, anyway." I remembered Oka. How deep did you have to scratch Jesse before he quit doing things the legal way?

He was quiet on the ride home. At the grazing lease he reined in. "You two go on ahead. I left a book here in the cabin I want to pick up," he said, but I figured he just wanted to be alone.

Lynne and I rode on in silence, letting the horses take their time. It had been a long day in a lot of ways.

We led the horses the last half mile home in the moonlight, holding on to the last few minutes of the evening, making them last. I wanted them to last forever because I knew this was all almost over. Beau's letter was in my pocket ticking like a time bomb. By tomorrow I should be gone. I'd never meant to stay this long and now I didn't *dare* hang around any longer. But leaving here would be the hardest thing I'd ever done. Because Lynne was here.

"Steve, talk to me." Her voice brought me back from somewhere far away. "What was in that letter, Steve? Ever since it came you've been acting like a stranger."

We were in the pasture above the barn now, high up on the hillside where the moonlight shone clear and unfiltered by the trees. There was one last gate to go through. We stopped and leaned on the fence instead. I looked into Lynne's face. Her eyes searched mine, looking for answers that weren't there. I *am* a stranger, I thought bitterly. That's all I'll ever be, a stranger on the run. "You don't want to know," I said. "There's a whole lot about me you don't want to know." But even as I said it I knew that she had a right to know. That I should have told her a long time ago. But I was so scared of losing her.

"No Steve," Lynne said softly, "you've got it all wrong. There's a whole lot I *do* want to know about you. I'm getting dangerously close to falling in love with you and that scares me. You're different than anybody I've ever known and maybe that's what I like about you, but you're also a puzzle I can't put together because too many of the pieces are missing." She reached out and took my hand. "Steve, please trust me. Tell me what's going on."

For a long minute I didn't say anything. I just stared

across the moonlight-blue hills and listened to the ripple of the creek below. Then, slowly, I turned back to meet her eyes. Maybe it was the mood I was in, the loneliness of knowing I'd be gone soon, or maybe the moonlight — and the fact that I was kind of dangerously close to falling in love with Lynne, too — but for the first time since I'd come here I let my guard down.

"I don't know where to start, Lynne." My voice came out low and ragged. "I've been in so much trouble . . ."

"I know," Lynne said gently.

I stared at her. "How do you know?"

"Kids who get suspended from school in grade seven and never go back don't usually spend the next few years studying in the public library."

"You checked that school registration form out pretty good, didn't you?"

"You bet," she said without a trace of guilt.

"I ran away. Things were too messed up at home. The bank had got the ranch a couple of years before and we had to move to Calgary. I guess that was the beginning of the end for me. I hated the city and I started gettin' in trouble at school all the time. Then Mom and Pop's marriage fell apart and she took my kid brother, Beau, and left. Then Pop fell apart and started drinkin'. When I finally got kicked out of school I decided it was time to run. Just crawled out the window and started hitchhiking west to Vancouver. I stayed there for seven years. I, uh, did a lot of stuff that was illegal, Lynne." I looked away to where the moonlit sea of hills washed up against the dark mountains.

"Are you running from the law, Steve?"

"Yeah."

"I thought so."

I'd been right all along. I *was* wearing a big sign that said, WANTED DEAD OR ALIVE.

"How'd you know?"

Lynne shrugged. "Little things. Like when I got that speeding ticket. I was mad but you were scared. Your hand was shaking when you handed me my driver's license."

"So if you knew, how come you still went out with me?"

Lynne reached up and gently turned my face so I had to look at her. "I went out with you because of who you are now, not what you were." She paused and swallowed hard. "I want to ask you what you did but I'm scared to hear the answer." The words came out just above a whisper.

Seeing the fear in her eyes hurt more than anything I'd felt in a long time. I put my arm around her shoulders. "All they want me for is breaking my day parole," I said. "I was doing time on a drug charge and when they let me out for a day I never went back."

Lynne sighed and I could feel her relax against my shoulder. "Well, if that's all it is you can go back, face up to it, and get it over with. You won't get that long a sentence for something like that. A few months in jail couldn't be as bad as spending the rest of your life looking over your shoulder."

"I can't go back to jail, Lynne. I'd never live to get out."

"Steve, I can imagine what being locked up must do to somebody like you. I could hardly stand it either. But you could handle it. Just for a few months if you knew you'd be free forever afterward."

I shook my head. "That's not what I'm talkin' about. I'm talkin' about *really* not livin' to get out. About wakin' up with a knife in my back some morning."

Lynne's eyes widened. "In jail? But with all the guards and security and everything . . ." Her voice trailed off.

I laughed bitterly. "Don't kid yourself, Lynne. Romero, the guy I used to work — run drugs — for *owns* the prison I was in, the one I'd get sent back to. He's got as many guys workin' for him inside as outside. When I was in, before I got busted delivering his dope, I was his boy. He was lookin' after me. Before I'd been in there two days I'd had an offer to keep me supplied with all the drugs I wanted and another guy had slipped me a knife to protect myself."

"So why would Romero get you killed now?"

"I set him up," I said, smiling at the memory. It was one of the few things I'd ever done that I was real proud of. "Got him busted. It was either that or kill him."

"Why?"

I felt the smile fade. "Because he killed somebody I loved."

"But if he's in jail now . . ."

"He never even went to jail that time," I said, the bitterness inside me seeping into my voice. "Guys like me go to jail. Guys like Romero hire the kind of lawyers that find a hole in the system for a snake like him to crawl out. He's already followed me to Alberta and tried to kill me once. The letter was from my brother. He found out Romero's on my trail again."

Lynne's face shone wet in the moonlight. "What are you going to do, Steve? I don't want to read in the paper someday about an unidentified body turning up in a ditch somewhere and know that it's you." She was crying now. Strong, tough-as-nails Lynne who drove like a maniac, made Ladysox behave like a lady, and who could stand up to everything from Mitch Williams to mad mama cows and never bat an eye, was crying for me. And that hit me kind of hard. Hard enough to melt the lump of ice that had been sitting in my chest for a long time now.

"Don't cry," I whispered. Then I kissed her. And this time when I closed my eyes I didn't see Tracey's face.

Twenty-three

I didn't leave the next day. I found a dozen excuses to hang around waiting for a miracle that would mean I didn't have to go. But the day after that there was another letter addressed to me. I didn't have any trouble recognizing the writing this time. I'd seen it on the board at school every day for five months. A kind of hollow feeling settled inside me. Why was Lynne writing me a letter? Why didn't she just come out to the ranch like usual? I tore open the envelope. The writing only covered half a page.

Dear Steve,

There isn't any easy way to say this. I won't be seeing you again. And it's not because of your past. Not the way you probably think, anyway. It's just that loving you hurts too much. I know that one of these days you'll just disappear and I'll never know where you went or if you're even alive. I can't stand hanging around waiting for that day so I'm going first. I'm leaving Rock Creek for the summer, maybe for good.

You'll always be someone special to me. Steve.
Love,
Lynne
P.S. Remember the good times.

I stood there in the hot sun by the mailbox staring at that piece of paper. She couldn't do this, But, she had. And everything she'd said was dead right. She'd done the best thing — for both of us — and I hated her for it. I crumpled up the letter and threw it in the ditch. I started to crumple the envelope, too, but something hard in the bottom stopped me. I reached in and brought out something small and gold that looked like it might have come off a charm bracelet. It was a Camaro.

It lay there in my hand shining in the sun. Remember the good times . . .

Choking back a sob I threw it into the tall grass at the side of the road.

And then spent the next hour finding it again.

Now it was time to go. Now that it was over with Lynne there wasn't much stopping me — until Jesse did. I was standing by the corral staring down the empty road and seeing a blue Camaro when he came up behind me. "Steve?"

I jumped. "You don't have to yell Jess. I ain't deaf."

Jesse pushed back his hat. "No?" he said with a grin. "Then how come I didn't get an answer the first two times I said your name?"

I shrugged. "I was just thinkin'."

"That must have been painful." Then Jesse took a good look at my face and his grin faded. "You okay, Steve?"

I nodded. "Sure. Why wouldn't I be?"

He didn't answer that. Instead he said, "I came to ask you if you'd come to the final hearing on the valley tonight. The more people that are there to support us the better."

I hesitated. I should be on the road. But, it was only one more day. And I owed Jesse. I nodded. "Sure Jess. I'll be there."

The community hall was packed with people. Just being there gave me a good case of claustrophobia. I remembered back when I first came here, I wouldn't even go to town in case I ran into somebody that recognized me. And then I went and got my picture on the front page of the paper.

Uneasily, I searched the crowd. My gaze settled on a man a few rows ahead. He had dark curly hair just like . . . My heart speeded up. Then the man turned to talk to his neighbor and I saw his face. Of course it wasn't Romero. What would Romero be doing at an environmental hearing? I asked myself. Looking for you, the answer came back. Restlessly, I shifted in my chair, wishing I was against the back wall where I could see everyone. People behind me made me nervous. But then the hearing started and my nervousness turned to boredom.

The hearing was just as boring as I'd expected it to be. A lot of dull people making a lot of dull speeches and listing off facts and figures until I just about fell asleep. I noticed that Carl *did* drop off once — and got rudely awakened by a jab from Connie's elbow. Jess, I thought wearily, you *owe* me for sitting through this stuff. I didn't even know where Jesse was. He hadn't come with us. Then, Jesse's name was announced and he stepped out from somewhere in the shadows near the back door. A ripple of interest ran through the crowd as he walked up to the platform.

He was wearing jeans and riding boots and a soft, almost-white buckskin jacket with beadwork patterns and long fringes that rippled when he moved. His hair hung in jet-black braids halfway to his waist. He looked ten feet tall up there on the stage.

Some busy little man in a suit scurried in to adjust the microphone to Jesse's height but Jesse ignored it and stepped to the side. His voice filled the room, deep and strong as the Wolfsong River.

"'As long as the grass shall grow. As long as the rivers run.' Those words were part of a treaty that the white man made with the native peoples of North America once. Those words were supposed to mean forever. Because no one could imagine a time when the grass no longer grew, when the rivers no longer ran. But now, less than a hundred years later, the time has come. Ask the Old Man River if it runs free now. Ask the pavement of the new subdivisions that spread like a disease over the hills around Calgary where the grass has gone . . . "

The words went on, sweeping across the room like the wind across the prairie. No one moved. No one whispered. No one even coughed. For the next half hour Jesse Firelight owned that crowd. He took them with him to the Wolfsong Valley. He showed it to them the way he had seen it. He made them believe.

"No, the Wolfsong Valley isn't Indian land. I have no ancient treaty to lay before you to prove that it can't be touched. It is no more my land than the rain forests of the Amazon are my land. It is no more my land than the old-growth forests of the Pacific coast are my land. Or the northern Alberta forests destined to be clear-cut to feed pulp mills are mine."

Jesse paused and stood looking out over the crowd for a minute. "And yet," he went on, his voice softer, "they're all mine." He stretched a buckskin-fringed arm toward the crowd. "And they're yours. There are some things that belong to everybody. And not just to the one species capable of destroying them. Places like the Wolfsong

Valley belong to you and to me and to every moose and bear and eagle and rainbow trout that needs the wilderness to survive. And once the wilderness is gone, and the wild things that live there are gone with it, we're not going to get it back. None of it. And it will only be a matter of time until we're gone, too.

"I read something in a book a long time ago and I never forgot it. It said that land is the only thing worth fighting for, the only thing worth dying for . . ." Jesse's voice went hoarse and I realized again how deep his feelings for that valley ran.

He stood silent for a minute, head bowed, trying to get his voice under control. Then, he raised his head and his eyes flashed defiance. "The Wolfsong Valley is worth fighting for. And worth dying for."

He turned and walked off the stage and back to his chair. And suddenly the whole crowd was on its feet, cheering and applauding.

If this had been a movie the scene would have ended there. But, this was real life. The hearing wasn't over. Another guy, in a suit, got up to speak. He turned out to be some high-priced consultant hired by the companies that wanted the development to go ahead. And he was good. He talked money. He talked unemployment, recession, the shortfall in government oil revenues the last few years, the billions of dollars of provincial budget deficit. And, he talked about how many millions of dollars of revenue the province would get if the Wolfsong Valley Project went ahead. How many schools it would build, how many hospitals . . .

None of it meant spit to me. Money ain't much good once you run out of air to breathe. But I wasn't on the board that made the decisions. They were all old guys, at least forty years old or more, in suits. And, from the looks of those suits, I figured money meant something to them.

The meeting ended and the board went away to live in expensive hotel rooms and think for a few days. I knew I should be out of here but I hung around waiting to hear the decision.

It came out on Friday. And, like everything else the government does, it didn't make any sense. Turned out the provincial government and the federal government were in the middle of a power struggle over which one got the final word on environmental stuff. The federal government wanted to study the situation some more. But the board belonged to the province and the board approved the project. Some high-level court was deciding on whether the federal government could delay it or not. But the bottom line was that, for now, the Wolfsong Valley belonged to the loggers.

Carl came home with the mail just as we were sitting down for dinner. He handed the letter to Jesse. Without a word, Jesse opened it, read it, let it slide through his fingers onto the floor, and walked out the door.

I started to follow him but Connie shook her head. "Let him go, Steve," she said softly.

When I went out after dinner I noticed that Firebird was gone so I figured Jesse had just gone riding to be alone for a while. I waited around all afternoon for him to come back. He didn't. He wasn't back when I finally fell asleep at two the next morning. And he didn't come back the next day either. Connie was going crazy worrying about him and I'd never seen Carl so quiet. And, for me, time just hung there waiting for something to kick it into motion again. I knew I should be getting out of here. Twice, I started to pack my stuff. But I couldn't go. Not till Jesse showed up. I started to see pictures of Firebird lying beside a badger hole, his leg broke, Jesse underneath him, his neck broke . . . Carl and Connie and I rode all over the ranch looking for him. I checked the cabin on the lease but he wasn't there.

The weather had turned hot and dry lately, with a relentless wind that stirred the dust and sucked the moisture out of everything. The wind got on my nerves. Everything got on my nerves. Where was Jesse? And where was Romero? How much further could I push my luck? I had to get out of here. But not until I knew Jesse was all right.

Friday, Connie and I were in the corral doctoring a wire-cut horse when Carl came back from the mailbox out of breath, waving a letter. Connie let go of the horse's foot so fast he almost fell on top of me. "What is it, Carl? Is it about Jesse?" she asked, her face gone pale.

"No," Carl got out between breaths. "It's *for* Jesse. Federal government environment department."

"Let me see that!"

Connie studied the envelope, held it up to the light, then . . .

"Connie! You can't — " Carl began but Connie had already ripped the envelope open.

"Sorry, Jesse," she muttered, "but I've got to know . . ." She read for a moment and then sucked in her breath. "Carl! Look at this. Now we've got to find Jesse!"

Carl read it and passed it on to me. Connie was right. Jesse *had* to see this. And then suddenly it hit me. If I'd been thinking halfway straight I would have known all along. There was only one place Jesse would go. I just hoped I wasn't going to be too late.

Twenty-four

Ten minutes later I was on Buster, galloping west into the wind, pushing the horse as hard as I dared. I had a long ride ahead of me.

It had never seemed so far before. The ride seemed to take forever but, in reality, it was still early afternoon when I pushed Buster up the long, dusty slope to the ridge above the Wolfsong Valley. The wind in our faces made the hill feel steeper. I pulled up the horse to let him get his breath.

Suddenly, there was a crashing in the brush just ahead. Buster threw up his head and whinnied. There was a loud answering whinny and Firebird came plunging out onto the trail, wild-eyed and sweat-lathered. He was saddled and the bridle reins were looped over his neck. As he slid to a stop beside Buster I reached out and caught him. And right then I caught my first whiff of smoke on the air. I was right. Jesse *was* camped up here somewhere and that was the smoke from his campfire. Firebird had just got away from him somehow. I'd take the horse back and Jesse would be there and I'd show him the letter and everything would be great.

So why was the hair on the back of my neck standing up and a big cold fist clenching my guts? I dug my heels into Buster's ribs and sent him charging up the trail at a dead gallop with Firebird at his heels.

The smell of smoke got stronger. My eyes were stinging as I pushed my winded horse around the last sharp curve and up the steep pitch to the top of the ridge. We slid to a stop in a cloud of dust and for a few seconds I just sat there, too stunned to move. Jesse's camp was here, all right, just off the trail. Lean-to with a bed of spruce branches, sleeping bag, spare clothes, and some cooking utensils, all neat and tidy just like Jesse always did things. But none of that mattered. Because Jesse wasn't there. And down below the valley was burning. A cloud of thick, gray smoke filled its whole south end, covering the destruction below with a blanket. A giant body bag for a murdered valley. Out of nowhere something I'd learned — memorized — in social studies flashed across my mind. Scorched earth policy. The Russians used it on the Germans back in World War II. Or was it against Napoleon a long time before that? Or maybe both. Saddam Hussein had done it when he retreated from Kuwait. It meant exactly what it said. When the battle was lost and you had no choice but to retreat you literally burned everything you had to leave behind. So the enemy got the land, but that's all they got. Scorched earth. No food. No shelter. No roads. No bridges. If you couldn't have it, you didn't leave it for them either.

Nobody would log the Wolfsong Valley now.

I saw Jesse's eyes again. The way they had looked when he finished his speech that night. ". . . land is the only thing worth fighting for, the only thing worth dying for."

Oh, God, Jesse, what have you gone and done?

I was so scared I couldn't think straight. If Jesse's

horse was still here, Jesse was still here — somewhere. "Jesse!" I yelled. "Jess! Where are you?" The only answer was the roar of the wind and the mocking laughter of the flames below. Without thinking what I was doing I slid off my horse, knotted the reins over his neck, and tied Firebird's reins up on his neck again. Horses and fire didn't mix. "Go on, get outa here while you still can!" I gave Buster a slap on the rump and he wheeled and broke into a run for home. Firebird was right behind him.

Well, now I couldn't go back — unless I wanted to walk and I hate walking. I started running down the steep trail into the valley. As I got lower the smoke thinned out and I could see the fire wasn't as big as I'd thought it was. It seemed to be centered on the clearing they'd dozed out to build the logging camp. Two big piles of knocked-down brush at the west end were totally covered by flames and the wind was whipping the fire from them into the surrounding trees and through the camp itself. A couple of trailers and a truck were already blazing fiercely and the fire was licking at the tires of another truck. There was no sign of life in the camp. There was no sign of Jesse.

My mind kept telling me to turn around and get out of there, back up on the ridge, as far away as I could get. But I just kept on running toward the fire. Jesse was down there somewhere. He had to be down there. Dead or alive, I had to find Jesse.

Suddenly something stopped me in my tracks. A sound that penetrated through the roar of flames and the rush of the wind. A high-pitched, whining sound. A chain saw. Somewhere down there, just beyond the flames, someone was running a saw. I started running again.

There were trees on fire on three sides of the camp now. The fire was cresting in the tops of the tall pines and leaping from treetop to treetop, lighting them like torches and leaping on to the next and the next. I had to get through the fire to reach the sound of the saw. It wasn't as bad as I thought it would be. Most of the fire was high above me and the underbrush was only burning in a few places. But I was plenty hot. Maybe the fact I'd been running flat out all the way from the top of the ridge had something to do with that.

I burst out of the fire and into the eastern edge of the camp clearing. The sound of the saw was dead ahead. Then, through the swirling smoke I spotted the figure of a man with a chain saw in his hands. Jesse. He didn't see me at first. He was too busy ripping through trees and brush, the big saw screaming in fury as it sank its teeth into living wood and spat out hot sawdust. I could see what Jesse was trying to do. He was cutting a wide swath ahead of the fire, felling the trees away from the flames and leaving nothing for the fire to feed on. But if he'd started the fire, why was he trying to stop it now? Maybe he'd meant to just burn the camp and the fire had got away. The reason didn't matter. I had to do something fast. One man couldn't stay ahead of the flames. Not in this wind. "Jesse!" I yelled at the top of my voice.

He swung around and saw me. He grinned, his teeth startling white against his smoke-smeared face. "About time you showed up, city boy. I need some help."

Before I could say a word he'd tossed the big saw in my direction. Out of sheer survival instinct, I caught it. He ran over behind a big fallen spruce and picked up another saw. He must have grabbed every saw in camp and brought them all over here. He jerked the starter cord and that one roared to life.

The saws howled in unison and trees fell, piling up like dead soldiers on a battlefield. The fire guard grew wider. But the flames were getting close. Behind us the camp was almost completely engulfed in them. An explosion shook the ground. Startled, I looked up to see a truck just a couple of hundred yards away explode into a giant fireball.

The pace of sawing trees down in the heat of the fire while breathing in more smoke than air was taking its toll. I started to cough and couldn't get stopped until I finally set the saw down and leaned against a tree, gasping for air. I saw Jesse had stopped, too, and was standing head down, panting. "What happened, Jess?" I gasped between breaths. "You try to burn the camp and the fire got away on you?"

His head came up. "You think *I* started this?" he rasped.

My eyes met his. "'Land's the only thing worth fightin' for, the only thing worth dyin' for'" I reminded him. "Was it worth burnin' out a logging camp for, Jess?"

Jesse's hand shot out and grabbed me by the collar. He slammed me back against the rough bark of the tree. "If you don't know me any better than that, city boy, you're even more ignorant than I thought." His voice was so hoarse the words came out barely above a whisper but his eyes blazed hotter than the fire around us, two points of light in a soot-black face.

For a few long seconds I stared back into those eyes and I read the truth in them. "Sorry, Jesse." My voice came out in a strangled whisper, too, partly because of the smoke and partly because Jesse was still doing a pretty fair job of choking me.

His hand relaxed on my collar and his face relaxed into a tired grin. "Don't be too sorry, Steve. The thought of burning the place did cross my mind once. But it was the camp garbage barrel that started this. The crew all went into town for the weekend and left this one genius to look after the place. First thing he did was light the garbage in a howling wind and then wander off for a nap or something. I saw the brush piles start to burn from the ridge before he even knew about it."

I looked around. "Where is he now?" I hoped Jesse hadn't thrown him in for a burnt offering or something.

"On his way back with a fire crew, I hope. I sent him off down the new trail in a truck for help."

I only had one more question. "What were you doin' here in the first place, Jess?"

Jesse grinned. "Just keeping an eye on my valley," he said. He reached down and picked up his saw. "Let's go city boy. Fire's gaining on us."

We were holding our own. Maybe we were even getting ahead a little. Jesse ran one saw out of gas, grabbed another, and kept cutting. Then a few minutes later, mine ran out of gas. "Got another saw Jess?" I yelled.

He shook his head. "Only had time to grab three."

"How about more gas?"

"Couldn't find any."

The wind was picking up again. The roar of the fire in the treetops was louder. Sparks were spattering on us like stinging raindrops. One saw couldn't finish the firebreak in time.

Jesse and I looked at each other and I knew he was thinking the same thing. His eyes scanned the half-burned camp and all of a sudden he grabbed my shoulder. "We've got one chance!" he yelled. He was looking at a big, shiny new D7 Cat, sitting at the clearing's edge, still untouched by the circling flames.

"Go start it up and start knocking over trees."

"Me? I don't know how to run those things. I just know how to wreck 'em."

Jesse's voice went scornful. "Aw, come on, city boy, any fool can run a Cat."

I shot him a defiant glare. "Someday, Jesse — " I began but he couldn't hear me over the roar of his saw. I gave up and ran for the Cat. I climbed into the cab and checked out the instrument panel. I could figure this out, all right. I'd just rather not have to do it with flames already hungrily licking the Cat's tracks.

Off-on switch *on*. Glow plugs button? Yeah, all diesel engines had them. Hold it in while you push the starter. Hey, no problem. Instantly the engine roared to life. Well, I thought grimly, surveying the encroaching circle of fire, no wonder it started easy. It sure was warm enough. I pulled a useful-looking lever and the blade lifted. Okay. Now, gear shift. Yeah, power shift on these things. I tried for first gear. The Cat crept forward. I found the throttle and jerked it wide open. The engine gave a roar like an enraged lion and we lurched full speed ahead. All right. We were in business. Except it might be useful to know how to turn — no steering wheel. That much I'd known. You steer these things with a set of levers. I pulled one. The right track stopped moving and the left one kept on going, taking us in a neat circle to the right. Got it! I moved the blade into position and started mowing a swath through the trees.

I can't say I did the world's neatest job but I sure did clear a path in a hurry. At least there was nothing there I wasn't supposed to knock down. Well, except for Jesse, that is. I did almost run over him once and he got pretty rude with his sign language about it. But it was his fault. He was a lot more maneuverable than a D7. It was up to him to stay out of my way.

Finally I cleared a wide space that ran all along the east side of the fire right up to the edge of the river. We just about had this fire stopped. Then I figured if I started pushing some of the already-burning trees back deeper into the fire it would run out of fuel even faster and we'd soon have it out. I roared right up to a tall fire-crowned spruce, knocked it down, and pushed it across the burn ing underbrush. That worked. I started to back out, dragging the blade, smothering the fire with it. There was a loud clanking noise and then all on its own, the Cat started turning in a circle. I threw it out of gear and took a look over my shoulder at the left track. It was fine. I checked the right one. It wasn't there. Well, it was sort of there. It just wasn't attached anymore. It had caught on a stump and now lay sprawled like a shiny metal snake as hot tongues of flame flared all around it.

I stepped to the door of the cab and looked out that side. There were a lot of flames there, too. Having the Cat throw a track here in the middle of the fire wasn't part of the plan. Through the wall of flames between us, I caught a glimpse of Jesse's face. He was yelling something at me. I couldn't hear a thing over the roar of the engine and the crackle of the flames but, reading his lips, I got something like, "Jump! You idiot!"

It was probably the best advice Jesse had ever given me. Suddenly, I knew how a circus tiger felt before he jumped through a ring of fire. But, I sucked in a deep breath — which turned out to be mainly smoke — and leapt through the flames. It was even hotter than I expected but I made it through. I stumbled and fell to my knees, struggled to my feet, and got instantly knocked over again by Jesse. It wasn't until he'd rolled me around on the ground for a while that I realized I'd been on fire in several places.

I looked back toward the D7. It was completely engulfed in fire now, its paint turning brown and blistering. "It died a martyr," Jesse said solemnly.

"Yeah," I croaked, "and it's about to have a Viking funeral. Let's get out of here before the fuel blows."

We'd just got safely out of the way when Jesse glanced up at the sky. "Here comes the cavalry. Just a little late as usual." I followed his gaze and saw it — no, _them_. Two big forestry choppers churning through the sky with water-bombing buckets dangling underneath them. Then I heard more engines, on the ground this time. Trucks coming up the new road behind us. And, eerie and out-of-place here in the middle of nowhere, the metallic sound of voices on two-way radios. The fire crew had arrived, just like Jesse said, a little bit late. The fire would still burn for a while but it wasn't going anywhere. Between the two of us we'd stopped it.

"Well, city boy." Jesse ran his blackened sleeve across his soot-covered forehead. "You gonna stick around for another hero cookie or you coming with me?"

I stared at him, confused. "Where you goin'?"

He nodded toward the ridge. "I've got a canteen full of ice-cold spring water up there. I don't know about you, but I sure could use a drink."

I nodded. "Let's go."

Jesse took a step, stumbled over a root, and almost fell. I threw an arm around his shoulders and we stumbled up the trail together.

It seemed like a long time later when we finally got to the top. Jesse found the canteen and we lay on the cool grass taking turns drinking and looking down at what was left of the Wolfsong Valley. Suddenly, I remembered something. "I got a letter here for you," I said, reaching to get it out of my shirt pocket. My hand touched something powdery. I looked down. My shirt pocket was gone, burned to a fine gray ash that disintegrated into nothing when I touched it. A few brown-toasted paper fragments fluttered away in the wind. I sighed, "Well, Jess, I had a letter for you right here in my shirt pocket."

"You don't even have a shirt pocket," he muttered, laying his head on the grass and closing his eyes. "Who was it from?"

"Federal government environment department."

Jesse sat bolt upright. "What did it say?"

"Think I'd dare open your mail?" I said, but I stopped kidding when I saw Jesse's arm muscles begin to tense. "But Connie opened it. It said that all development in the valley was prohibited for the next five years while they did in-depth environmental studies."

Jesse stared at me. Then he turned to look out across the valley. "They were a little late, weren't they?" He started to laugh. But a minute later the laughter turned into sobs. He buried his head in his arms and cried like he'd been saving up the pain for a long time. I laid my hand on his shoulder and sat looking out over what was left of the Wolfsong Valley. The ragged black gash in the forest still bled wisps of smoke. The angry whine of chain saws still ripped the air as the fire crew felled the last of the smouldering trees. Above, the choppers still pounded relentlessly through the air, circling, waiting to pounce on any flame that dared to raise its head.

The valley would never be the same. It had been hurt, its wild innocence gone. But from up here the blackened patch didn't look so big.

I turned to Jesse. He had stopped crying and was looking across the valley, too. "She'll heal, Jess," I said softly. "She'll be scarred up a little but she'll survive."

We all would.

Epilogue

---

*T*he next day I was running again but at least this time I wasn't going to be broke and on foot. I had a couple thousand dollars saved up. I asked Jesse to drive me into town so I could buy a car. He gave me one of those see-right-through-you looks of his. "You seeing dust on your back trail again, city boy?" he asked.

This time I just nodded. "Yeah, Jess, it's time I was gone."

I was afraid he was going to start asking questions or try to talk me out of going but he just sat staring into my soul for a while and then got in the truck. We headed for the used-car lot in Rock Creek.

I was kicking tires on a half-decent Dodge when Jesse gave a low whistle. "Next horse I get I'm going to call Jaguar," he said, his voice full of awe and admiration.

Jesse didn't make a whole lot of sense sometimes, I thought, still studying the Dodge. Then, all of a sudden, I felt the hair on the back of my neck stand up. *Jaguar?* I followed Jesse's gaze to the service station across the street. There, pulled up at the pumps, sat a gleaming black Jaguar with B.C. plates. A dark-haired guy was leaning out the window, talking to the gas jockey and somebody real big was in the passenger seat. For a second I froze solid. Then, feeling like I was in one of those dreams where you can't make yourself move any faster, I opened the door of Jesse's truck and got my jacket off the seat.

"Jesse?" I said softly, my voice feeling just as frozen as the rest of me. "I've gotta get out of here. Now. Tell Carl and Connie thanks for everything and I'll write and explain to them."

Jesse stared at me like I'd lost my mind. His gaze drifted across the street and then back to me. "Romero?"

I met Jesse's eyes. "Yeah." I held out my hand. "Thanks for everything, Jess." I tried hard to swallow the lump in my throat as our hands met in a farewell grip. I turned away but Jesse stopped me.

"You're not going to walk, are you, city boy?"

"Well I sure ain't about to stand here dealin' on a car till Romero sees me. Yeah, I'm walkin'."

Jesse shook his head. "No, you aren't." He reached into his pocket, brought out his truck keys, and handed them to me. "Now get going."

In spite of everything I couldn't help but grin. "Told you once I wasn't stupid enough to steal *this* truck."

Jesse grinned too. "But you're not stupid enough to look a gift horse in the mouth either."

"I can't take . . ."

"Get in," Jesse growled.

I climbed in and turned the key. The engine wheezed to life. As I started to pull out of the parking spot Jesse raised a hand to stop me. "There's an ancient Indian secret you need to know about this truck," he said solemnly. "When the red needle starts to close-dance with the big E, add gas."

STODDART BOOKS YOU'LL ENJOY

Picture Books

King of Cats	Vlasta van Kampen & Arthur Johnson	7737-2589X
The Sign of the Seahorse	Graeme Base	7737-26101
A Dark, Dark Tale	Ruth Brown	7736-73717
Mademoiselle Moon	Marie-Louise Gay	7737-26535

Junior Gemini, Ages 8–11

The O-Team	Darcy and Duanne Jahns	7736-73784
Death Drop	Mary Blakeslee	7736-73210
And the Boats Go Up and Down	Wilma Alexander	7736-7344X
Five Days of the Ghost	William Bell	7736-73687
The Refuge	Monica Hughes	7736-73776
Home Base	Judy Peers	7736-73466
It's Up to Us	Carol Matas	7736-73350
Terror in Winnipeg	Eric Wilson	7736-73695

Irwin Junior Fiction, Ages 8–11

Oliver's Wars	Budge Wilson	7737-5508X

Gemini, Ages 12 and Up

The Leaving	Budge Wilson	7736-73636
Absolutely Invincible	William Bell	7736-72915
Don't Worry About Me, I'm Just Crazy	Martyn Godfrey	7736-73644
Riptide!	Marion Crook	7736-73628
Dreamspeaker	Cam Hubert	7736-73768
Sandwriter	Monica Hughes	7736-73768

Irwin Young Adult, Ages 12 and Up

Brothers and Strangers	Marilyn Halvorson	7737-53699
Stranger on the Run	Marilyn Halvorson	7737-55322
Beyond the Dark River	Monica Hughes	7737-55225
Foghorn Passage	Alison Lohans	7737-54962
Between Brothers	Irene Morck	7737-55306

Non-fiction, All Ages

What Time Is It?	A.G. Smith	7737-24990
Free Stuff for Kids	Edited by Sylvia Hill	7737-2642X